PUFFIN BOOKS

The Sands of Time
A New Hermux Tantamoq Adventure™

Praise for *Time Stops for No Mouse*, the first Hermux Tantamoq Adventure™

'Highly original . . . Think Niles Crane as a talking mouse in a Hitchcock script and you'd be about right'
– TONY BRADMAN, *DAILY TELEGRAPH*

'An endearing mixture of romance, adventure and mystery [and] sharp modern wit'
– *FINANCIAL TIMES*

'A slick, unusual and sophisticated tale. Talking animals usually leave me cold but this is different . . . a marvellous, twisting and turning detective story. Time flies with this one . . . A real find'
– *IRISH TIMES*

'Watch out, Stuart Little, you have a literary rival . . . This pleasurably anthropomorphic story has bags of charm [and] a zesty plot'
– *GUARDIAN*

'A chic, distinctive, offbeat thriller'
– *OBSERVER*

'I have a new hero. It is Hermux Tantamoq . . . I cannot commend my new hero and his author highly enough'
– *BOOKSELLER*

PUFFIN BOOKS

Published by the Penguin Group
Penguin Books Ltd, 80 Strand, London WC2R 0RL, England
Penguin Putnam Inc., 375 Hudson Street, New York, New York 10014, USA
Penguin Books Australia Ltd, 250 Camberwell Road, Camberwell, Victoria 3124, Australia
Penguin Books Canada Ltd, 10 Alcorn Avenue, Toronto, Ontario, Canada M4V 3B2
Penguin Books India (P) Ltd, 11 Community Centre, Panchsheel Park, New Delhi – 110 017, India
Penguin Books (NZ) Ltd, Cnr Rosedale and Airborne Roads, Albany, Auckland, New Zealand
Penguin Books (South Africa) (Pty) Ltd, 24 Sturdee Avenue, Rosebank 2196, South Africa

Penguin Books Ltd, Registered Offices: 80 Strand, London WC2R 0RL, England

www.penguin.com

First published by Terfle Books 2001
Published in the USA by G. P. Putnam's Sons,
a division of Penguin Putnam Books for Young Readers 2002
Published in Great Britain in Puffin Books 2003

1

Text copyright © Michael Hoeye, 2001, 2002
The Sands of Time Map © The Pinchester Company, LLC, 2002. Used by permission.
A Hermux Tantamoq Adventure is a trademark of Terfle House Limited.

The moral right of the author has been asserted

Set in Cochin

Made and printed in England by Clays Ltd, St Ives plc

British Library Cataloguing in Publication Data
A CIP catalogue record for this book is available from the British Library

ISBN 0–670–91307–3

THE SANDS OF TIME

A HERMUX TANTAMOQ ADVENTURE™

MICHAEL HOEYE

PUFFIN BOOKS

Hermux Tantamoq Adventures
by Michael Hoeye

Time Stops for No Mouse

Acknowledgements

Many, many thanks to my creative family at The Pinchester Company, LLC. To David Vogel, Larry Fulton, and Jean Gillmore. Thanks again to the remarkable talent and dedication of booksellers everywhere. You are extraordinary people. Without you the world would be dull and dark indeed. Thanks to my wife, Martha Banyas, for her unwavering trust and inspiration. To my mother, Lily, for getting me off to a roaring good start. To my sister, Patricia, for her kindness (and for the teasing too). And to my friends for putting up with my wackiness for all these years.

Write to us at hermux@hermux.com

This book is dedicated to a lifetime
of unforgettable teachers

PATTY SMITH

FAYE LEEPER

JACK FRYAR

NAOMI LEBOWITZ

VINCENT MARIANI

STANLEY ELKIN

ANNELISE MERTZ

MERCE CUNNINGHAM

JACQUELINE SCHUMACHER

EUGENE MONICK

PHYLLIS TRIBLE

ANN BELFORD ULANOV

GEORGE W. S. TROW

Chapter 1
DO DROP IN

'What a beautiful morning for watchmaking!' thought Hermux Tantamoq as he unlocked the door to his shop. There was something delicious in the air. He wrinkled his nose and sniffed. His whiskers twitched. He took a deep breath.

'Ripe apples,' he said. 'Now that's a nice smell!'

He sniffed again. Hermux was a mouse who appreciated a good meal. A nice, plump red apple might be just the thing for lunch. With a thick slice of Cheddar cheese. And a crusty piece of bread. What a pleasant thought! He raised the shade and switched on the lights. He put a sign out on the front counter that said, *I'm back in the workshop. Please ring the bell!*

He took off his emerald-green woolly coat with the bumble-bee buttons and hung it on a hook. Then he rolled up his sleeves and went to work.

Hermux got Clenton Yooger's big pocket watch down from the work shelf. All it needed was a good cleaning. He fitted his magnifying loupe to his right eye and opened the heavy gold case. First he removed the winding stem. Then he inserted a tiny pair of tweezers to release the main spring, which, as everyone knows, is the very most ticklish part of watchmaking. That's when someone slapped him on the back.

'Tantamoq!' a shrill voice boomed in his ear.

Clenton Yooger's main spring sprang from his watch, skittered across the workbench, ricocheted off the tool rack and disappeared on to the floor.

'Say! You're not Tantamoq!'

'I am too!' said Hermux.

'Tantamoq is older. He's my age!'

Hermux rubbed his eyes and studied his surprise visitor. It was an old chipmunk. He was bit taller than Hermux, as you might expect, but so skinny that he couldn't have weighed much more than a mouse. He was wearing a faded, rusty-coloured corduroy jacket with patches on the elbows. And the shoulders. And the lapels. And the cuffs. Some of the patches even had patches.

Hermux thought chipmunks were a clownish lot in general. But this one looked particularly odd to him. There was even something sort of lopsided about his head. Hermux smiled to himself. Then he noticed that the old chipmunk was missing an ear. It was completely gone. Like someone had snipped it off with a pair of scissors. Hermux winced. 'Ow!' he thought. 'That must have hurt!'

'I am Tantamoq!' Hermux told the old chipmunk. 'Hermux Tantamoq.' He extended his paw. 'You must be looking for my father, Linnix. This was his shop. I took it over when he retired.'

'Of course,' said the old chipmunk. 'Your father. He's the one I want to see! Where can I find him? I want to see him right away.'

'I'm sorry, but that's not possible.' Hermux stopped. 'My

2

father passed away several years ago.'

'Linnix!' sighed the old chipmunk. 'I didn't know. I'm so sorry.' Suddenly he seemed confused and uncertain.

'Well, maybe I can help you,' said Hermux.

'I doubt it!' said the old chipmunk, shaking his head violently. 'I must be cursed! I need a watchmaker with a solid grasp of history. Not a beginner.'

'I'm not a beginner, and I'm very interested in history,' argued Hermux. 'Just this summer I did a walking history tour of South Glemmon. I visited the very factory where the first twisty watchband was invented. Ask me anything about watches.'

'I need somebody who understands mechanics. Who knows how to put pieces together and figure things out. Someone who's not afraid of complications.'

'Well, that's me in a nutshell!' said Hermux. 'I am certified to repair cuckoo clocks of all sorts. Even the great antiques from Grebbenland. And they are really complicated, I can tell you that for sure!'

'This involves more than clocks and watches, my boy! I need somebody with heart.'

Hermux recalled the image of a bold young mouse standing before her gleaming silver aeroplane. It was Linka Perflinger, the renowned adventuress and aviatrix that he had met in the spring of that year. Hermux had nearly lost his life rescuing Ms Perflinger from the clutches of a sinister plastic surgeon, Dr Hiril Mennus. In the process he had lost his heart to the dashing Linka. But in the end she had chosen someone else.

'I have heart,' he said ruefully.

'The point is that I need somebody just like your father.'

3

'I'm a lot like my father,' said Hermux. He glanced up at the photograph over his workbench. It was a smiling picture of Linnix Tantamoq at the National Convention of Watchmakers. He had just been named Watchmaker of the Year. Hermux drew himself up. 'Like my father,' he said proudly, 'I'm not afraid of complicated problems. And I can solve them under pressure. Perhaps you heard about my involvement in the Perflinger case?'

'No. Why would I?'

'Why, it was in all the papers! Earlier this year. My picture was printed several times. Along with Ms Perflinger and Tucka Mertslin and Ortolina Perriflot! You can't say you didn't hear something about it. Hiril Mennus? The Beauty Doc Murders? Where have you been?'

'I've been working! In the field! I don't have time to waste reading newspapers! And I couldn't get them if I did!'

'What do you do?' asked Hermux.

The old chipmunk jerked back suddenly and narrowed his eyes, his one ear cocked and alert.

'Why do you want to know?' he asked suspiciously.

'Well, it sounds like you've got a problem. An interesting one. And I'd like to hear about it. What can I do to help you?'

'You can start by helping me get this off,' the old chipmunk grumbled. He pointed to the tattered knapsack on his back.

'Boy, this is heavy,' said Hermux, wrestling it on to the workbench. 'What's in it?' He started to unbuckle it.

'Hey!' snapped the old chipmunk. 'Keep your hands off! I'll do that!' He pushed Hermux away.

Hermux watched his irritable visitor rummage about in his knapsack. Time had certainly not been kind to the old guy. He looked run-down and run over. From his patched jacket to his

4

threadbare pants and his dusty, scuffed boots. His fur was thin and lifeless. His paws were nicked and scarred. And then there was the missing ear. How had that happened? He certainly didn't look like any friend of his father's that Hermux had ever met. And Hermux couldn't quite picture his father being good friends with a chipmunk to begin with.

The old chipmunk interrupted his thoughts.

'If you'll have some patience for an old man's cautious nature,' he said, 'I've got something very interesting to show you. It's a very puzzling object that I acquired recently. It raises several questions about history. Questions that would have interested an intelligent, imaginative watchmaker like your father. Maybe they will interest you.'

A noisy clanging in the front of the shop interrupted him.

Chapter 2
THE 'A' LIST

Someone was pounding the bell on the counter.

'Looks like you made the list, Hermux!'

It was Lista Blenwipple with the morning mail.

'And not everybody did. I can tell you that for a fact!' she continued with great satisfaction. She appeared in the door of the workshop. 'Oh, here you are!' she said cheerily. She handed Hermux a handful of mail.

The new issue of *Watchmaker's Monthly* was right on top of the autumn catalogue from Orsik & Arrbale, the department store. On its cover an athletic young field mouse was shown leaping in midair from a towering stack of hay. He was wearing a very catchy outfit – pumpkin-coloured shorts and a thick grass-green sweater covered with bright yellow exclamation points. There were bills and notices. And there was a letter from Nip Setchley. Hermux started to open it.

'Oh, that's not it, silly!' cautioned Lista. 'It's not mixed in with the everyday mail. No, indeed!' She removed a pale grey envelope from a special inside compartment of her mailbag and held it up before him like some sort of trophy.

'There are those that were chosen. And those that weren't,'

she went on mysteriously. 'I know some people who are in for a big disappointment – people who ought to know better than irritate me by putting on fancy airs – people who'll be sorry that their mail was unavoidably detained in transit.'

Finally she handed Hermux the envelope. 'It looks like you'll be going.'

'Where?' asked Hermux.

'Don't be ridiculous!' Lista burbled. 'To Mirrin's opening at the museum, of course! What has everybody in Pinchester been talking about since August? Honestly, Hermux, I wonder sometimes if you're entirely there . . .'

Hermux examined the envelope. It was addressed to him in a beautiful flowing script written in dark blue ink. He opened it carefully and withdrew the invitation.

The Department of Modern Art of the
Pinchester Museum of Art and Science
requests the honour of your presence
for the gala opening of

LOST & FOUND
THE VISION OF MIRRIN STENTRILL

New Paintings

October 20   8 p.m.

Formal Attire • Dinner • Dancing • R. S.V. P.

Hermux was awfully proud of his elderly friend Mirrin. After three long and difficult years of blindness, she had regained her eyesight. That was barely six months ago. She had returned to her painting studio immediately, and since then she had created a remarkable series of paintings of the disturbing visions she had had during her blindness. It had been Hermux who had restored her sight. And that had come about as a result of his surprising adventure with Linka Perflinger, Dr Mennus, and Hermux's neighbour, the irrepressible and ruthless cosmetics tycoon Tucka Mertslin. But that is another story.

'Of course, you being Mirrin's good friend, there wasn't much doubt that you'd get invited,' Lista confided. 'But you can never be completely sure. Take Lanayda Prink for example. She donates her entire collection of coffee mugs to the museum, including all the mugs from all her trips out West, and does she get invited? Something tells me she won't. And boy, will she be steamed! It shows that you can never be too polite to your postal worker.'

She winked.

'And now, Hermux, who is your interesting new friend?' she asked.

Hermux turned to make the introductions. But the old chipmunk was gone. He had sneaked out of the shop without making a sound.

'I'm afraid I don't know his name,' said Hermux. 'A nervous, odd fellow. He says he knew my father. But he didn't say how. I never found out what he wanted. I don't even know where he's from.'

Hermux ran the tip of his paw thoughtfully over the workbench where the old chipmunk had set his knapsack.

'Although from the looks of this sand, I would say that until recently he's been out West. Probably in the desert.'

Chapter 3
WHO'S IN CHARGE?

'I don't care how famous she is!' the mayor shouted into the telephone. 'I don't care if she was blind! I don't care if she was the first mouse on earth! I will not have obscene art at the Pinchester Museum. It won't happen! And that's that! I'll take the place apart brick by brick and sell it for scrap. Tell that to the board of directors!' He slammed the receiver down with a bang.

Hooster Pinkwiggin was not a wood rat to be trifled with. He had a vicious temper, especially during election years, and a tendency to snap first and ask questions later. Several of his assistants had the scars to prove it. One by one they scooted back as he glared at them in a fury.

'Paintings of cats!' he screamed. Unable to reach a single assistant, he grabbed a pencil off his desk and bit it in two with a sharp snap. That seemed to calm him for a moment. But not a long one.

'Is the woman completely mad? Does she want to frighten everyone to death with her nonsense? Is she some sort of sick publicity hound? Pinchester is a civilized city! We don't speak about cats in public. We don't read about them in books. We're certainly not going to show paintings of them in the museum!'

'Mmmmh ... Mayor Pinkwiggin?' interrupted an earnest-looking squirrel with an unusually bushy tail.

'Yes?'

'There seems to be one more problem with Miss Stentrill's portraits of cats.'

'Now what?'

'Apparently they're nude –'

'Nude?' exploded the mayor. 'Nude?! How can cats be nude when no one has ever seen one to begin with? How can they be nude when they never even existed? What kind of wacko nut is this Stentrill woman?'

His lips curled up in an ugly snarl. The assistants took bigger steps further back. The mayor grabbed the telephone cord with his front teeth. The powerful muscles in his jaws flexed. Then he remembered the nasty shock he'd got the last time he'd bitten through a lamp cord.

'I won't stand for it!' he screamed. The telephone went flying.

'I will not be made a fool of!' he bellowed.

'They'll be sorry they tangled with me!' he roared.

'This is war!' he screeched. His legs went stiff with rage. He began to turn himself around and around in his swivel chair. Faster and faster.

'Close the museum immediately!' he thundered as he came around the first time. His feet sent the desk lamp flying.

'Lock it!' he cried, spinning by. The photos of his wife and his children and his rowing boat fell over with a crash.

'Bar the door!' he snarled. Coffee cups spilled their coffee.

'Chain it!' he blared. Sugar cubes rolled from the sugar bowl like dice.

'Nail it shut!' he croaked as he slowed to a stop. 'Arrest

everybody inside!' A tower of carefully typed reports leaned and swayed back and forth, back and forth.

'Mayor Pinkwiggin, I'm afraid that's going to be more difficult than you think,' explained the squirrel, who eyed the teetering stack of reports hopefully. He had been up half the night working on those reports, and getting the pages in the right order had been harder than you'd think.

'You're new here, aren't you?' asked the mayor, sitting up in his chair to get a better look at the squirrel.

'Yes, sir! I am!' said the squirrel.

'And your name?'

'Birbir, your honour,' he said proudly. 'Birbir Nifftin.'

'Well, Birbir,' said the mayor, leaning forward over his desk. 'Why don't you explain to me exactly what the big difficulty is.'

'Well, sir,' Birbir began. The other assistants took shelter behind whatever furniture they could find. Birbir himself was trying to back towards the door but discovered that the long fur on his tail was somehow twisted up in the mayor's chair. 'The problem is the museum. You see, the city doesn't own the Pinchester Museum. The museum owns it. It's actually private property. We can't tell them what to do.'

And that really was too much for the mayor, especially during an election year. He launched himself at Birbir with his teeth flashing and nipped him right on the arm.

'Ouch!' squeaked Birbir. 'That hurt!'

Birbir's tail whipped spastically, and the mayor's chair unspun like a wild top. It threw the mayor against his desk, scooted across the floor, knocked over the water cooler and bounced out of the window. It landed with a loud crash on the mayor's new car three floors below.

'We'll see who owns the Pinchester Museum!' panted the

11

mayor. 'We'll just see about that!' He pounded his desk furiously with both fists.

And with that, Birbir's leaning tower of carefully typed reports finally came tumbling down.

Chapter 4
EMERGENCY MEETING

'Order! Order!'

Durrance Pootinall rapped the gavel on the conference table.

'The emergency meeting of the board of directors of the Pinchester Museum of Art and Science will now come to order,' Durrance announced.

But nobody listened.

'Shut up!' he shouted. 'Shut up! Shut up! Shut up!'

The noise died down.

'I want to know what's happening!' demanded Elusa Loitavender indignantly. 'I'm so embarrassed! I've hardly been out of my home for two whole days. I get dirty looks everywhere I go. From people I don't even know. Even my cook is talking about it. I just hate it! I hate scandals. I hate them. All of you know that. And tonight! Protesters! Here at the museum! What is happening?'

'We'll get to that, Elusa,' Durrance assured her. 'But I see that the refreshments have arrived. All in favour of a brief break before we get down to business please say "Aye!"'

'Aye!' shouted the board of directors. They jumped to their

feet and raced to the doughnut cart as Lanayda Prink rolled it through the door.

'Jam doughnuts!' chirped Flurty Palin, and heaped several of them on to a saucer. 'This is swell. Really first-rate.'

Elusa reached delicately for a plain cake doughnut.

'Mmmm,' she said. 'These are quite fresh!'

Lanayda beamed with pride. She was so nervous that she was afraid she might wet her pants. Part of it was standing face-to-face with the richest people in Pinchester. But most of it was anticipation that the museum board of directors was going to formally announce the bequest of her coffee mug collection and maybe unveil plans for an extravagant new gallery to house it. 'The Lanayda Prink Wing of Decorative Arts,' she thought dreamily. 'And to think it all started with a single mug at the gift shop on the first day of my first trip to Glinkrivvin Canyon. I wonder if I should start by telling them about the picnic we had that day? I'd made boiled egg and dandelion sandwiches. It was so bright outside, and I had forgotten my sunglasses, so I ran into the gift shop to buy some. And just inside the door there was a little shelf of the cutest little mugs. I remember looking at them and thinking it would be so nice to have one for a conversation piece at the coffee shop back home. And it was so hard to decide which one. They were all so sweet and –'

Durrance rapped the gavel sharply and woke Lanayda from her dream. The board members had returned to their seats. A broad trail of doughnut crumbs led back to the conference table. And someone had spilled cream all over the cart and not wiped it up.

'To begin with, we all owe a word of thanks this evening to Lanayda Prink.'

Lanayda took a deep breath and started towards the

14

conference table. This was her moment. She clutched the short speech she had written and practised that afternoon. She decided right then and there that she would definitely start with the story of the picnic. It would have been just perfect if she had thought to make boiled egg and dandelion sandwiches for tonight. But they had asked for doughnuts.

'A word of thanks for excellent doughnuts on such short notice,' said Durrance.

Lanayda smiled and nodded. But no one was watching her.

Everyone was watching Flurty Palin. He had crawled up on to the table and was squeezing the jam out of a jam doughnut to draw a big strawberry-coloured heart on the conference table. Inside it he scrawled *Flurty + Elusa 4ever.*

Elusa covered her eyes and squealed, 'Stop it, Flurty! That's awful! You know it's not true!'

Durrance's patience was getting thin. He rapped the gavel again.

'Thanks for coming, Mrs Prink. Don't worry about the doughnut cart. Just leave it for now. You can pick it up tomorrow.'

Lanayda was frozen in place. She had already unfolded her speech, and now she stood there absentmindedly motioning with it towards the table.

'Just leave the bill on the cart,' Durrance told her with an understanding smile. 'Really,' he thought. 'Just a bit pushy about the money, aren't we?' Then he indicated the door with a brisk nod. 'We've got to be moving along, Mrs Prink. Thanks again! And don't forget the regular board meeting at the end of the month. You have no idea how much we appreciate what you do.'

Lanayda walked quietly to the door and left. She was a very disappointed woman.

'And now, let's get down to business,' said Durrance seriously. 'Mr Palin, will you please return to your seat while Ms Denteel calls the roll.'

Birkanny Denteel, the oatmeal heiress, made a great show of uncapping her gold fountain pen and opening her notebook. She had very beautiful paws, long and slim with elegantly tapered claws. They were her best feature. Except for her oats. Holding a spoonful of steaming hot cereal, Birkanny's paws appeared on every box of Denteel's Delicious Oats.

'Dr Vannerly Parrunk?' she asked, directing a graceful paw towards him.

'Present,' answered the director of the museum, who was a small but dignified harvest mouse.

'Flurty Palin?'

'Mmmmph!' answered the notorious playboy through a mouthful of strawberry jam.

'Skimpy Dormay?'

'Present, of course,' said a very thin and very elegant vole. She wore a simple black velvet suit set off by an extravagant necklace of gold and silver peanuts.

'General Forthgen?'

'Present and accounted for,' barked a fat little house mouse. The general was still vigorous and commanding despite his advanced years. However, he was somewhat deaf on occasion, particularly on occasions that suited him.

'Hinkum Stepfitchler the Third?' Birkanny enquired with great seriousness.

There was no answer.

Around the whole conference table there was a distinct pause in doughnut chewing.

'Hinkum Stepfitchler the Third?' repeated Birkanny anxiously.

All heads looked about.

'I am here,' answered a very solemn, very carefully groomed mouse. He put down the enormous book he was reading. 'I'm sorry,' he explained without sounding the least bit sorry. 'I'm afraid I'm a bit preoccupied with this latest translation of mine.'

'Don't worry, darling,' Elusa Loitavender reassured him. 'Nothing has happened. Go back to your work. It's far more important than this. If anything does happen, I'll tap you on the shoulder.' She directed an irritated look at Durrance. 'I, for one, was under the impression that this was an emergency meeting ...'

Durrance took the hint.

'Ladies and gentlemen of the board, we shall conclude the roll call. All present signify by saying so.'

'Present,' responded the others.

'Madame Secretary, please so note. Now, as you all must know, we have the serious business of the Mirrin Stentrill show to attend to. But before we do that, I would like to introduce our newest addition to the board – one of Pinchester's most illustrious tycoons and our newest patron of the arts, Ms Tucka Mertslin.'

Chapter 5

Motion on the Floor

The door opened quietly, and in walked Tucka. She was very modestly dressed. Nothing arched or dangled. Nothing clinked or clanked. Nothing flashed or beeped. There were no moving parts. There were no wires that corkscrewed. No feathers that waved. No stripes. No polka dots. No plaids. She wore a straight, slim floor-length gown that called very little attention to itself. No accessories. No jewellery. She was simple. She was pure. She was nothing less than the new and improved Tucka Mertslin.

Tucka was happy. She loved rich people. They were so much fun. They were so full of life. And they had so much money! She took her seat at the table and looked around, riffling her whiskers and sniffing the air with appreciation. She could practically smell the money in the room. She knew she was going to like this. Even if it meant sitting at the same table with Ortolina Perriflot, who, as far as Tucka was concerned, was a sneaky little Goody Two-shoes, even though she was probably richer than all of the others put together.

Tucka smiled at Ortolina and waved at her. Ortolina waved cautiously in return. With Tucka you could never be sure.

'Thank you for joining us, Ms Mertslin,' Durrance

continued. 'We're in a crisis here, so I'm afraid you'll have to dive right in. Now, Dr Parrunk, what's the status on the Stentrill exhibition? What's the fastest and easiest way we can cancel it? What do we have to fill in with? And how in the world did you get us in this awful mess to begin with?'

Dr Vannerly Parrunk rose to his feet. 'Now, now, let's all calm down. Things aren't that bad. If you'll recall, when you hired me to take over the museum, my orders were to breathe some life into the place. Get people involved. Get people talking about art ... and we've done just that!'

'But we'd like them to say nice things,' Elusa interrupted. 'And the things I've heard about this show are just awful. C-A-T-S! I can't even say it! It's vulgar and nasty! And I'm ashamed to be a part of it! I won't be a part of it. I want the show cancelled. Tonight!'

'What do we have for backup?' asked Durrance.

'The only thing we've got is the Prink Collection,' Parrunk explained.

'Coffee cups?' Skimpy Dormay asked indignantly. 'You expect me to dress up for a gala opening of coffee cups? Get that thought right out of your head!'

'May I speak a moment?' asked Ortolina Perriflot. 'It was only as a favour to our community and a very personal favour to me that Miss Stentrill even consented to this exhibition. It is an important show by one of our greatest artists. Mirrin's work poses bold questions. Tonight the question for us is whether we have the courage to consider the answers.'

'Very lofty sentiments, Ortolina. Very grandly put.' Hinkum Stepfitchler III closed his enormous book and addressed the board in a smooth, melodious voice. 'But there are other questions for us to answer. Is this a museum or a circus tent? I have been led to believe that this is, in fact, a museum of art and science. Is it art to show lewd and terrifying pictures? Is it science to study the existence of non-existent creatures? This show is neither art nor science. It's nonsense. And nonsense of the worst, most destructive sort. Images of cats! Is this your idea of providing a stimulating cultural life for the citizens of Pinchester? If I had been consulted earlier, I could have saved us all the enormous embarrassment and expense of cancelling the show. Which is what I suggest we do immediately before it's too late.'

'Hear! Hear!' cheered Elusa. 'I motion that the Mirrin Stentrill exhibition be cancelled.'

'Do I hear a second?' asked Durrance Pootinall.

'Seconded,' said Hinkum.

'Count the votes!' Elusa gloated.

'All in favour?'

Elusa's paw shot up. Followed by Hinkum. And Durrance. And two more.

'All opposed?'

Ortolina raised her hand. Dr Parrunk raised his. Skimpy Dormay raised hers. She had already bought her dress. Flurty raised his paw. Elusa shot him a dirty look. He lowered it.

'What's happening?' demanded General Forthgen noisily.

'We're voting!' explained Elusa. 'You should have raised your hand earlier. We don't want C-A-T-S in the museum!'

'I'm not afraid of them!' boasted the general. 'Leave 'em to me!'

He raised his hand and waved it vigorously.

Then Flurty raised his hand again. Big museum openings always meant heaps of food set out on great big platters. Elusa scowled at him. But this time he ignored her.

20

'We have a tie vote,' cautioned Durrance.

'But I haven't cast my vote yet,' said Tucka in a very soft voice. Everyone's eyes were suddenly on her.

She leaned close enough to Ortolina to whisper. Their last encounter, in Dr Mennus's secret laboratory at the Last Resort Health Spa and Research Clinic, had been less than cordial. Tucka had not behaved well at all.

'This evens us up! OK? A clean slate?' Tucka asked.

Ortolina nodded reluctantly.

Tucka raised her hand very slowly.

'Opposed,' she said.

'Ladies and gentlemen,' Durrance announced, 'we seem to have an exhibition.'

Chapter 6
DRESS UP

'Terfle! I'm home!' cried Hermux. He closed the door to his apartment and ran to his study.

Terfle, his pet ladybird, roused herself from her late-afternoon nap. The day had completely slipped away from her. She opened her shell and fluttered her wings slightly. It was a half greeting–half yawn.

'I've got a surprise for you!' Hermux told her. He set down his armload of shopping bags and packages. 'It's a present.'

He held up a small box wrapped in marigold tissue paper and tied with a bright red bow.

'I stopped by the pet store on the way home. I hope you like it.'

Terfle made a leisurely inspection of the box and signalled her approval by tapping her perch lightly with her antennae.

'All right, then!' Hermux carefully untied the bow and removed the tissue paper. He folded it carefully and set it on his desk. Then he held the box close to the cage and with a great flourish he removed the lid.

Terfle's eyes, which had a tendency to look a little beady, took on a sudden lustre. Hermux lifted the present delicately from the box. He opened the cage door and set it inside on the floor. It towered over Terfle.

'Well? What do you think?'

Terfle stood completely motionless.

'Of course it's not real,' Hermux apologized.

Terfle was too astonished to respond.

'It's a rosebush,' said Hermux.

And it was. A jewelled rosebush. Although they weren't real jewels. But it had real thorns and real leaves made of gold. Although it wasn't real gold.

Terfle approached the bush and began to climb. She climbed up into its branches. She crawled out on to a leaf. She strolled around a bud. Then she settled on a voluptuous open rose. She nestled down into the centre of the blossom. It was a small bed of yellow diamonds. Although they weren't real diamonds, they were still very sparkly.

Terfle was overcome with emotion. There was so much to explore. So many places to hide. Even if it wasn't a real bush, it was the most beautiful thing she had ever seen. Hermux had taken her by surprise. She had no idea how to respond. She opened her crimson shell to its widest extension, showing its bold black markings. Then very, very slowly she closed it and looked up at Hermux with what she hoped he realized was genuine devotion.

'You look very beautiful there,' Hermux told her. 'Oh my goodness! Look at the time! I've got to get dressed for Mirrin's exhibition.' He grabbed his parcels and disappeared into his bedroom.

Twenty minutes later he re-emerged.

'Do you think this looks good on me?' Hermux asked uncertainly. He stood in front of Terfle's cage and turned slowly so she could see his tuxedo from every angle. It was his first tuxedo, and it was expensive.

Terfle turned on her perch and walked towards the wall of her cage so she could get a better look at him. She stared at Hermux thoughtfully. As a ladybird she was naturally partial to polka dots. So the big diagonal stripes put her off at first. But she liked the shininess of the satin, and the bright pink and green were very pleasant colours to her eyes. Although personally she thought black and red were more appropriate for formal evening wear. Overall, though, she thought he looked very nice. And the stripes did make him look a little thinner.

She ruffled her wings a bit in approval.

'Thanks,' he told her with a little bow. 'My first museum gala opening! I hope I don't make any big mistakes.'

Hermux looked at his watch.

'I've got to rush to pick up Mirrin!'

Terfle butted her head against the bars of the cage.

'Now, don't wait up for me. It could be a very late evening. There's dinner and dancing.'

Chapter 7
PERIPHERAL VISIONS

Mirrin answered the door in a rust-coloured evening dress that contrasted handsomely with her silver fur. She laughed happily at the sight of her young friend dressed in bright pink and green satin stripes.

'Hermux!' she exclaimed. 'Why ... that is the most ... I mean ... you look absolutely ... perfectly ...' Mirrin had to stop a moment to catch her breath. Tiny tears were gathering in the corners of her eyes. 'Hermux! You're a dear!'

'I look funny, don't I?' asked Hermux, disappointed. 'Maybe you should go alone.'

'Nonsense! You look charming! Really. Like a bright piece of candy! I'll be the envy of everyone there! Now come with me. We're not late yet, and there's something I want to give you. Tonight is the perfect time.'

Mirrin led him back through the house to the door of her painting studio.

'Now,' she said, 'cover your eyes. I don't want you peeking.'

Hermux kept his eyes tightly closed as she led him inside. They were greeted by the warm smells of fresh turpentine and paint. A wave of happiness swept over Hermux, starting from

25

his toes and stretching to the tips of his whiskers. He remembered many evenings sitting here talking with Mirrin about her work during the three years that she was blind.

At first she had tried to keep painting.

'I still see,' she had told him. 'What I see is darkness. But it's not empty. It's dense and tangled like a forest. It's fascinating. I want to paint it.'

She had tried valiantly. Carefully and methodically she had arranged her brushes by size and her paints by colour. Then she had set to work, but it had been difficult. She could see what she wanted to paint. She couldn't see her own efforts to paint it.

While she struggled, the dark forest came to life. Mirrin began to catch glimpses of movement. Shadowy creatures lurking in the background. Then creeping closer. And closer. As though they were stalking her. Great furry faces filled the void. They made her uncommonly anxious. Cold, watchful eyes watched her. Monstrous mouths. Gleaming fangs. Claws curved to rip and tear.

Again and again she tried to capture what she saw.

Hermux worried about her.

'What do you see?' she would ask him anxiously as he stood before a new canvas that she had struggled over for days. 'Can you see what I'm talking about? Can you see what it is?'

But all Hermux could see were fractured lines and smears of paint. Mirrin endured the disappointment and frustration until one day she finally gave up and left her studio for good.

Now, unexpectedly and thanks to Hermux, she had returned to it. The studio felt alive again.

'I haven't ever thanked you properly for what you did,' Mirrin began. 'You saved me, Hermux. You saved my life and my work. There's no way I can ever repay you. Ever. Or even begin to say what your friendship means to me. I only wish your mother and father could have lived to see what a very fine and brave mouse their son grew into.

'OK,' she said with a deep breath. 'Open your eyes!'

Hermux found himself standing in front of an easel. On the easel was a portrait of him. Full length. Almost life-sized.

Mirrin had painted Hermux standing in the door of his shop, as he often did, looking out at the street. She had captured him accurately. He didn't look quite slim, but not especially fat. His ears weren't large enough to be noble. His nose was too small to appear refined. And his eyes seemed just the slightest bit off-centre.

But she had also captured him with affection. The Hermux in the portrait may not have looked as brave as a soldier or as dashing as a movie star. But he looked like a mouse you could trust. A kind, cheerful and intelligent mouse. A good and caring friend.

The portrait was a true gift from one generous heart to another. This time the tears that gathered were in the corners of Hermux's eyes. He stood up taller in his pink and green tuxedo.

'I look like a very decent mouse,' he told Mirrin happily.

'You are a very decent mouse, Hermux,' said Mirrin. 'And much, much more besides.'

Chapter 8
A Face in the Crowd

When the taxi rounded the corner of the museum, Hermux and Mirrin both gasped. A line of police cars blocked the street. The pavements overflowed with people, pushing and shoving their way towards the museum. Some of them clutched invitations. Some of them were yelling. Some of them held big signs. Some were climbing over the fence and trampling the flower beds.

"What on earth is happening?" asked Mirrin.

"Some nut's art show," said the driver, stopping the car. "It's been nothing but trouble all day. You want out here or you want me to get closer?"

The crowd surged towards them.

"Watch out!" shouted Hermux. He and Mirrin shrank back as the taxi was engulfed in a crush of bodies and paws and faces.

Suddenly, through the window, Hermux thought he recognized a familiar figure. It was the old chipmunk who had visited his shop. He was being pushed along in the crowd.

"Mirrin, look!" said Hermux. "It's the old chipmunk!"

Hermux knocked on the glass to get his attention.

"What chipmunk?" asked Mirrin. "Where?"

'The chipmunk who came to the shop! The one who knew Dad and needed help.'

'What are you talking about?'

'Right there!' Hermux said. 'Him!'

But the chipmunk was gone. The crowd had pushed on, and he was lost to sight.

'Where did he go?'

'WHO is HE?' demanded Mirrin.

'An old chipmunk. He said he was a friend of Dad's. He has some kind of important mystery to solve. And that's all I know. He walked into the shop last week. And then he ran off. And he never even told me his name.'

'A chipmunk?'

'Yes.'

'Your father's age?'

'That's right.'

'What did he look like?'

'Pretty run-down. Skinny. Kind of nervous. And he's missing an ear.'

Someone rapped on the window.

'Mirrin!'

It was Dr Parrunk from the museum. He opened the door and extended his hand to her.

'Thank goodness you're all right! Let's get you through this crowd,' he said. 'The mayor is holding a press conference. It would really help if you'd take some questions from the reporters and try to calm people down before this really gets out of control.'

Chapter 9
MEET THE PRESS

Hermux stayed close to Mirrin as Dr Parrunk led them through the crowd. He didn't like the feeling in the air. There was something ugly and threatening about it. It didn't feel like Pinchester at all. Hermux was alert and suspicious and protective of Mirrin.

He shielded his eyes from the spotlights and flashbulbs as they stepped out of the crowd and started across the broad museum steps towards a makeshift podium.

'It's the cat woman!' someone shouted.

'And a clown!' someone added.

'Go, girl!' somebody encouraged.

'Go, clown!' somebody added.

'Yeah! Go back where you came from!'

That ignited a mixed chorus of hisses and boos and hurrays.

'Shut up, everybody!' The mayor's voice boomed through the loudspeakers. 'I'm not finished!'

The crowd quietened down.

'In conclusion,' he concluded, 'I leave you with this question: is this what we want to call art in the fair city of Pinchester? Is this what we want hanging on our public walls?'

'No!' shouted the mayor's wife. And all of his assistants. And a lot of the crowd.

'Yes!' shouted the mayor's son. And all of his friends. And all of the people with invitations in their hands who were trying to get up the steps and into the museum.

The mayor smiled at his wife. He nodded at his assistants. He waved at the crowd. He glared at his son.

'Remember me on Election Day! A vote for Hooster Pinkwiggin is a vote for Pinchester!'

Loud applause. The mayor's assistants rushed forward and patted him on the back.

Dr Parrunk took the podium.

'Ladies and gentlemen and members of the press,' he began, 'Miss Stentrill, the artist, is here tonight and would like the opportunity to answer your questions.'

'You would?' Hermux whispered to Mirrin.

'I would not,' Mirrin whispered back. 'But I guess I will.'

Mirrin stepped behind the podium. Hermux thought she looked very beautiful there. Her silver fur shone brilliantly in the spotlight and her dark eyes appeared especially sharp and intelligent.

'Good evening,' Mirrin said pleasantly into the microphone. She had taught children for too many years to be nervous in front of cranky crowds.

'Miss Stentrill!' a voice called out. 'Cartin Polenspook, the *Weekly Squeak*. Are you saying that cats exist?'

'If you mean "do they exist as actual creatures?" No. I'm not saying that.'

'Are you saying that we're descended from cats? Are cats the missing link?'

31

'A missing link to what?' she asked.

'Mirrin! Mirrin!' yelled gossip columnist Moozella Corkin. 'Can you comment on rumours about the seances? Are you really in contact with a three-thousand-year-old cat spirit?'

'I am a painter. Not a spiritualist. There are no seances in my home. And no cat spirits —'

Cartin Polenspook interrupted. 'I'm not following this. You don't think cats exist. You don't think they ever did. You're not channelling cat spirits. Then why on earth did you paint these paintings?'

'There's a misunderstanding here,' answered Mirrin. 'I've never said that these are paintings of cats. I don't know who said that. But what if they were cats? We're taught as children not to think about cats. Never to speak about them. Never even say the word. But we do think about them. And we talk about them. At least we whisper about them behind closed doors. The fact is that the idea of cats is real. It lurks in every one of us. It slinks about in the shadows. It stalks us on sleepless nights. It pounces when we least expect it. It toys with us when we're anxious. It bats us about when we're feeling helpless. And maybe you think it's obscene even to mention the idea of cats. But I don't agree. Being blind taught me one thing at least. Whatever we can see in the light, no matter how bad, is less frightening than what we can imagine in the dark. I'm not trying to upset anyone. Darkness can be very scary, that's what I'm saying. And I'm trying to make some sense of the fear.'

'Are you saying that mice are inferior creatures?' a thin, raspy voice broke in.

Mirrin peered over the podium to see who was speaking. A short, middle-aged mouse pushed his way to the front. He carried a sign.

```
┌─────────────────────────┐
│    100% MOUSE           │
│         &               │
│    PROUD OF IT!         │
└─────────────────────────┘
```

'Are you saying that mice are inferior creatures?' he repeated. He was shaking with anger.

'I don't understand you,' answered Mirrin. 'How do you get that?'

'Fear! Fear! That's how! Why should we be frightened? Where's your pride?'

'I didn't say that we *should* be frightened. I said that sometimes we *are* frightened. And with my paintings, I'm trying to look fear in the face.'

'You're pathetic! That's what. Pathetic! The mouse is the oldest and noblest of earth's creatures. No animal is more nimble, more intelligent, or more adaptable than the mouse. Mice invented language. We invented civilization. We invented culture. Mice invented art! We invented museums! Mice built this museum! And what do you give us in return? Fear!'

Mirrin was speechless.

The angry mouse raised his sign high over his head.

'It's time for mice to be strong!' he shouted. 'To assume our natural dominion over the earth!'

A sturdy white rat reached over and punched him in the nose.

And pandemonium broke loose.

Chapter 10
SPIN CYCLE

A fat hamster in a flowered housedress rammed the podium and sent it crashing.

'Run for it!' Dr Parrunk told Mirrin and Hermux. He led the way, and the three of them scampered up the steps towards the museum's great revolving door.

A stampede followed. Noisy grunts and squeals crackled through the loudspeakers.

The mayor's son got to the door first. Followed by the mayor's assistants. Followed by the mayor and his wife.

'Hurry up! Hurry up!' barked the mayor. 'Move it!'

There was only one son. And he was fast. But there were ten assistants. The senior assistants insisted on going first. And that caused confusion. The confusion caused a tangle. The tangle caused a blockage. And the blockage stopped the door.

That's when the mayor nipped Birbir Nifftin right on the bottom. Birbir kicked out his powerful hind legs, and the door spun so fast that the senior assistants were thrown right back out of the museum, down the steps and into the mob.

The mayor hesitated. But not his wife. She leapt through the door with the athletic skill of someone who never missed a white sale at Orsik & Arrbale. The mayor took a deep breath, closed his eyes and ran forward.

He made it through. His tail didn't. It wasn't quite broken. But it was severely kinked.

Mirrin and Hermux and Dr Parrunk were next.

'Bar the door!' Dr Parrunk shouted to the guards as soon as they were safely inside.

'Are you all right?' Hermux asked Mirrin.

'I think so,' she said. 'Nothing seems broken. So far it's certainly more exciting than my last show.'

'Hey! Where are the cat paintings?' a loud little voice interrupted them. 'I want to see them!'

It was the mayor's son.

'Wow!' he exclaimed, pointing at Hermux. 'That's a neat suit!'

'Noose! Get over here!' snapped the mayor. 'We're leaving right now. We don't like these people.' He sniffed the air appreciatively. 'Hmmn! I smell food, though! Roasted peanuts for sure!'

He rubbed the kink in his tail thoughtfully.

'Say, since we're already here, maybe we should look around a little before we go. You! Birbir! Find out how to get to the buffet!'

Chapter 11
SHOW TIME

The museum's Great Entry Hall had been specially decorated for Mirrin's show.

'It's breathtaking!' Hermux said.

The floor was covered with a thick layer of hay. The towering marble columns had been wrapped with quilted crêpe paper and transformed into ears of fresh corn that extended in tasty-looking rows as far as you could see.

'I could lie down right here and just stare at the corn.'

'I think we'd better keep moving,' Mirrin told him. 'Or I'll miss my show. Look! There's Ortolina! Doesn't she look beautiful?'

A smiling Ortolina Perriflot welcomed them at the entrance of the exhibition. She was not, in fact, what most mice consider beautiful. She was much too tall to be beautiful. And too unconcerned about it.

'I'm so relieved you're all right,' she said. She gave Mirrin a warm hug. 'Hermux, you're looking very festive as usual. It's good to see you both.'

The three of them were bound by a special relationship. They had shared an unusual adventure that year. Ortolina was the only person besides Hermux who knew the secret of Mirrin regaining her eyesight.

'I got here early,' Ortolina went on. 'I've never seen people this excited about anything, much less art. Everyone wants to meet you, Mirrin, of course.'

She wasn't exaggerating. Ortolina didn't usually exaggerate. As the richest woman in the world, she didn't have to. People were lined up inside the gallery to meet Mirrin Stentrill and get her autograph.

But nobody wanted Hermux's autograph, and he soon found himself alone in the gallery.

Hermux approached the first painting cautiously. Even from a distance he felt a cold stab of fear. Luminous, slanted eyes stared out from the canvas. They seemed to follow him as he threaded his way through the crowd. They were curious and calculating eyes set in an enormous, blunt face covered with impossibly long silver-blue fur.

It was a primitive face. No snout to speak of. Just a broad, flat muzzle with the most horrifyingly savage mouth. It had hideous little front teeth that would be no use at all for gnawing or nipping. And horrible, gigantic fangs on either side.

Without looking directly into the creature's eyes, Hermux walked up close to the painting and examined its teeth. The fangs were longer than his arms.

'It would be hard to eat with those things in your mouth,' he thought. 'Maybe cats weren't so dangerous.'

'I can't believe anything with teeth like that could possibly have fur,' said a dark grey mouse next to him. 'I believe she's got it all wrong. If there ever were cats, they were obviously scaly creatures. Like lizards and snakes.'

'I think they look rather nice the way they are,' said a black otter in a bright red vest. His smile revealed a rather impressive set of his own teeth.

The dark grey mouse scowled up at the otter and then turned away. 'Come on, honey!' he said, pulling his wife through the crowd. 'I didn't realize they let otters in this museum. They're not even rodents, and now they act like they own the place.'

'Of course ...' The otter stopped to scratch briefly behind his ear. 'Cats had no culture. They never learned to use tools, apparently. Or even how to swim. And from what I've been able to glean from the scanty information that's available, they were very dirty and had an awful smell. Simply unbearable. That probably would have done them in eventually. Even if the meteor hadn't fallen.'

'What meteor?' asked Hermux.

'Why, the meteor that destroyed the island they lived on. Don't you know anything about cats?'

'I guess I don't.'

'Oh, the island thing! That's sheer nonsense!' interrupted a brown rat impatiently. 'My wife is extremely good friends with the artist. She knows the whole story. These cat creatures live on another planet. They communicate with Mirrin through an old radio. The pictures are totally fake. She's not permitted to show us what they really look like. Once they decide if we're friendly or not, they'll send a spaceship to visit us.'

'You people have no idea what you're looking at! Do you?' an angry voice burst out. 'Are you completely stupid?'

It was the old chipmunk.

'Why, it's you!' said Hermux excitedly. 'Where have you been?'

38

The old chipmunk stared in disbelief at Hermux's pink and green tuxedo.

He started to speak, but at that moment a loud gong sounded.

A silvery mole in a forest-green uniform announced, 'Ladies and gentlemen, dinner is now served!'

'It's about time!' shouted Flurty Palin. He broke into an immediate run for the exit. The crowd followed instantly. And in moments the gallery was empty.

Except for Hermux and the old chipmunk.

Chapter 12
Chow, Darling!

Flurty Palin was invariably the first person to arrive at any buffet table. So he was more than a little surprised to discover that this time the mayor and his family had got there ahead of him. Flurty was also more than a little miffed to see the mayor and his family skimming the best parts off practically every dish. That was something he usually did.

'Say!' said Flurty, trying to reach around the mayor. 'Leave a little of that cheesy crust on those potatoes, will you?'

The mayor ignored him.

'Flurty!' Elusa Loitavender called from a table near the dance floor. 'Come sit with us!'

Flurty scooted ahead of the line and snatched an entire walnut whipped cream pie right from under the mayor's pudgy paw.

'Now, Flurty,' Elusa warned when he sat down. 'You have to promise to behave. Birkanny and Skimpy and I are here to have a nice evening. Nothing silly. And remember that you promised me a dance.

'There's Hinkum,' said Elusa hopefully. The distinguished mouse of letters stood at the entrance, watching the party with

40

the undisguised look of someone who had seen it all before and hadn't found it especially amusing the first time.

Hinkum Stepfitchler III was the last living member of the greatest dynasty of scholars and inventors in modern mouse history. And he looked the part. Moody, bored and imposing. He was dressed offhandedly that night in a dark blue smoking jacket, although naturally he didn't smoke.

Hinkum was there because his presence in high society was required. But Skimpy knew that he would prefer to be at home, working in his library, in the great old Stepfitchler mansion, nestled in its own private park in the centre of the campus of Stepfitchler University.

Hinkum was brilliant. He was also rich, elegant and aloof. It was a combination that Elusa found completely irresistible. She motioned for him to join them at their table.

'And there's that Mertslin woman!' she said, pointing towards Tucka. 'What on earth is she wearing? And what happened to her fur?'

Chapter 13
ALONE AT LAST

'Why did you disappear on me?' Hermux asked the old chip-munk.

'I had second thoughts about getting you involved.'

'But you never really gave me a chance. If you'll explain the mystery, I'd be glad to help you. At least if I think I can. And if you don't want to talk about that, would you at least tell me how you knew my father? I don't often meet any of his old friends.'

'Your father and I hadn't been in touch for many years.'

'So why now?'

'Because of these,' said the old chipmunk.

'The paintings?'

'Exactly,' he said. 'And not exactly.'

'I see,' said Hermux, but he really didn't.

'Your father and I had some trouble with cats when we were in college. Pretty serious trouble,' he said ruefully. He rubbed his missing ear.

'You don't mean that cats did that!' Hermux exclaimed.

'No,' sighed the old chipmunk. 'But it was because of cats. It was all because of cats. The whole darn thing.'

'You know, I don't even know your name.'

'I'm sorry,' he said. 'I've lived alone so long that I've completely forgotten my manners. My name is Birch. Birch Tentintrotter. Your father was my very good friend. I'm so sorry that he's gone.'

'He never talked about you,' said Hermux.

'I can't blame him,' said Birch. 'I was nothing but trouble for your father. And for Mirrin.'

'You know Mirrin too?'

'Once upon a time, I knew her very well. We were engaged to be married.'

It made Hermux very angry to hear that. Mirrin and a chipmunk? It just wasn't nice to think about.

'That's a lie!' snapped Hermux without thinking how it sounded.

'No,' Birch said very quietly. 'It's the truth. The very sad truth. That's why it was important for me to come back to Pinchester.'

'Well, have you talked to her?' Hermux demanded.

'No. I'm ashamed for her to see me like this.'

'Like what?'

'Like this. Old. Poor. Broken-down. I'm nobody. And look at her. Look what she's done. Look at these paintings!'

'What about these paintings?' Hermux asked. 'They still scare me a little. Mirrin has told me all about them, but I still don't really understand. Are the cats real? Where are they? And how did they hurt you?'

'It wasn't cats that hurt me, Hermux. It was my theory of cats. That's what did it. My theory of cats caused me to disappear. But hold on a minute. What's that fellow there doing with Mirrin's painting?'

Hermux turned and saw at the far end of the gallery a short, middle-aged mouse standing in front of one of the paintings. It looked like the man who had started all the ruckus at the press conference. He was standing on his tiptoes with a big paintbrush in his hand. He was painting a black moustache on the face of a fierce-looking calico cat.

Birch leapt into action. And Hermux was right behind him.

'Stop that, you vandal!' Hermux yelled.

The mouse turned and ran for the exit. But Birch headed him off and brought him down with a flying tackle.

'Take your filthy chipmunk paws off me, you miserable excuse for a rodent!' the mouse cried in a fury. 'Let me go! Get away from me!'

Hermux wrestled the paintbrush from his hand.

'And you!' the mouse hissed at Hermux. 'Have you no pride in yourself? What kind of a mouse are you?'

'Actually, I'm quite proud. Especially right now,' Hermux answered. 'And if you really want to know, I'm a house mouse on my father's side. Mostly field mouse on my mother's side. And you know what kind of mouse you are? You're a bad mouse! That's what kind!'

He shook his finger at the mouse.

'If you'll hold him,' Hermux told Birch, 'I'll go get help.'

Moments later Hermux came back with a portly guard, who handcuffed the angry mouse. Then, putting one heavy foot on the end of the mouse's tail, he told him to get up.

'Now, what's going on here?' the guard demanded.

'Look what he did!' Hermux exclaimed, pointing at the defaced painting. 'He ruined it.'

The angry mouse scrambled to his feet, breathing hard. Suddenly he ran at Birch and Hermux.

44

'I'll ruin you!' he shrieked.

But when he got to the end of his tail, he was stopped short. He fell flat on his face.

'I'll make you both pay for this! Don't think I won't! I'll find you, and I'll make you sorry!'

'We called the police,' Hermux said. 'They'll be here in a minute.'

'In that case,' Birch confided to Hermux, 'I think I'll be going. I never seem to get along very well with the police. I'll come by your shop tomorrow. We'll talk then.'

Then Birch scurried across the gallery and vanished through the door.

'Hey! Where's he going?' demanded the guard.

'Uhh ... he had to go to the bathroom,' Hermux explained. 'He'll be right back.'

Chapter 14
FLY GIRL

Tucka Mertslin's dress was covered with flies. Thousands and thousands of them flapped their iridescent little wings, making rainbows shimmer up and down her floor-length strapless gown.

All eyes were on her. Tucka turned slowly so the dress could be viewed from every angle. She had bleached her fur snow-white and combed it straight back. The effect was dazzling, and she knew it. She couldn't help smiling.

The chemists at Tucka Mertslin Cosmetics had worked for weeks to perfect Tucka's Shoo-Fly Fashion Glue. It had cost her a fortune. But judging by the buzz that swept the party, it was going to be a grand success. Tucka was making her move into fashion. If she had her way, every woman in the room would be wearing Shoo-Fly Shoes by the end of the year. Not to mention belts, purses, hats and scarves in every colour imaginable.

Moozella Corkin made a beeline for Tucka. She knew news when she saw it.

And Tucka knew opportunity when she saw it. She blew an air kiss at Moozella and gave her dress a little shake to wake up the flies. Moozella had her notebook out and was already scribbling. Tucka was just about to give Moozella an exclusive scoop on colour breakthroughs at the Mertslin Fruit Fly Breeding Programme when a young voice broke in.

'Doesn't that hurt the flies?'

It was young Noose Pinkwiggin.

Tucka ignored him. She winked at Moozella.

'I think that's cruel,' said Noose. 'You're torturing those flies. Just look at them. They're miserable.'

Tucka bent down to speak to Noose.

'Don't be silly! They're not miserable. They're having fun!'

'No!' said Noose. 'They're not. You're having fun. I don't like you.'

A crowd had gathered to see what Tucka and the nice young boy were talking about.

'Well, dear, the boy does have a point,' a well-dressed matron interjected. 'It really does seem like cruelty to animals.'

'Cruelty?' Tucka's eyes flashed. She shot a worried look at Moozella. Moozella was taking notes as fast as she could write.

'I think cruelty is a bit harsh,' Tucka said mildly. 'These flies have a life expectancy of only twenty-four hours. So short. So limited. Can you think of a better way for them to spend it? I'm exposing them to art. I'm introducing them to society. These are probably the first flies that ever set foot in this museum.'

'Well, I don't know about that, I'm sure,' the matron responded.

'Let me ask you this,' Tucka said with a razor-thin smile. 'Do you allow flies into your home?'

'Of course not! Don't be ridiculous!'

'Well then, let's not be so quick to cast the first stone!'

47

Tucka turned away, taking Moozella firmly by the arm and moving towards the buffet table.

'If there's anything I can't stand, it's hypocrisy,' she whispered to Moozella. 'Incidentally, you're looking awfully good tonight. Have you lost weight?'

Chapter 15
THE WINGS OF LOVE

Hermux found Mirrin at Ortolina's table.

'I need to talk to you,' he whispered. 'Right away.'

'Of course,' said Mirrin. 'But there's someone here who wants to say hello to you.'

'Hermux, it's wonderful to see you! How are you?'

Hermux turned and found himself looking into the warm, friendly eyes of Linka Perflinger.

'Adventuress, daredevil and aviatrix,' Hermux said to himself dreamily.

'Linka!' he said to her. 'Linka! I'm ... I'm very happy. I'm surprised. I mean, I'm happy to see you. I'm surprised to see you here. How are you?'

Hermux had seen Linka only four times in his entire life. None of them were under the best of circumstances. All of them barely six months ago. But Linka Perflinger's bright face and indomitable spirit were permanently engraved on his heart.

'Have you been travelling?' Hermux asked eagerly.

'Not so much,' she said with a slight frown. Then she laughed. 'The wedding plans, you know.'

'Ah, yes,' Hermux sighed. 'The wedding. Have you set a date?'

'It all depends on Turfip's schedule. He's leading another expedition for the Perriflot Institute. But the departure date isn't definite yet.'

'Will you be going on the expedition?'

'Not on your life!' a hearty male voice answered for her. Turfip Dandiffer, PhD, had joined the conversation. He was a robust-looking mouse in a rumpled tweed jacket that had a little patch on each elbow.

'Turfip Dandiffer, PhD,' he said, extending his large paw. 'And you are?'

'Hermux Tantamoq.'

'Oh, yes. Hermit. Of course! The watchmaker.'

'Hermux. Not Hermit. I'm not a hermit, as you can see. If I were a hermit, I wouldn't be here,' said Hermux with a little laugh.

'No. Of course not,' said Dandiffer, a bit puzzled. 'Well, Hermit, as I was saying, expeditions are no place for a woman. Besides, my little winged warrior is coming down to earth. Aren't you, darling? Hasn't Linka told you? She's hanging up her wings!'

'You're giving up flying?' Hermux asked Linka in disbelief.

'Just for the time being. Turfip's terribly busy at the Institute,' Linka explained. 'I'm trying to help get his office organized so he can concentrate on his work. He lost his assistant this year in Teulabonari. And things have got into a bit of a mess, haven't they, honey?' She poked at Turfip playfully.

'Poor Glower!' said Hermux. 'It was awful what happened to him.'

50

'What was I thinking?' apologized Linka. 'Of course you know the whole story. You were practically there.

'Sweetie,' Linka asked Dandiffer, 'did you ever thank Hermux for saving your journal this spring?'

'Probably not,' he said. 'Would you mind doing it for me? Ortolina wants to talk to me. Then I think we should go. It's getting late, and I've got a very early meeting.'

He kissed her on the cheek.

'Nice seeing you again, Hermit.'

'Turfip is a bit forgetful,' Linka explained when he had gone. 'But he's really very sweet when you get to know him. And he's brilliant.'

'I'd say he's forgetful,' thought Hermux. 'He also forgot to thank me for saving your life.' But that wasn't a very nice thought, and Hermux tried to put it out of his mind.

'There's so much to do. I just don't have time for adventure right now. Turfip is being considered for a position at the university. So we'll be entertaining a lot. The plan is to sell my plane and put the money towards a bigger house. Mine is just too small for the both of us. And I can always get another plane when we're more settled,' Linka said. Hermux thought he detected a slight note of doubt in her voice.

In fact, he thought he detected a slight note of doubt in Linka in general. There was something subdued about her. She had lost the air of urgency that had made her so unforgettable.

Still, Hermux had no intention of ever forgetting her.

'Well, Turfip is waving at me. I've got to go,' she said. 'It was lovely seeing you. I would love to talk some more sometime. You haven't told me a thing about you.'

'How is your wristwatch?' Hermux asked.

51

'Oh, it's perfect,' she said, holding out her arm so Hermux could see it. 'It keeps perfect time. To the second.'

'That's good to hear,' said Hermux with a smile. He blushed.

Linka leaned forward and kissed Hermux lightly on the cheek.

'Thank you, Hermux!' she said. 'I owe you my life. I'm very happy. Really, I am.'

Hermux touched his cheek where she had kissed him and watched her wistfully as she walked away.

Mirrin tapped him on the shoulder.

'Are you OK?' she asked.

'Oh. Sure. I guess. Maybe. Not really. I'm not. I'm miserable. What should I do?'

'You said you needed to talk to me.'

'Oh. Right! I did. I did. I met Birch Tentintrotter. The chipmunk. The one I was talking about.'

'Hermux!' Mirrin said in a shocked tone. 'Don't say that!'

'It's all right. I know all about you and Birch. He told me. And I admit I was shocked at first. But you broke it off. And that was the sensible thing to do.'

'Stop it, Hermux! Stop it!' Mirrin cried.

'What's wrong?'

Mirrin burst into tears. Hermux handed her his handkerchief, eyeing her nervously.

'Do you still love him? Is that it?' Hermux asked, not really wanting to know the answer.

He liked Birch well enough. But chipmunks were a little flighty as a rule. The fact was that mice just didn't marry chipmunks. Not in Pinchester, anyway. And while Mirrin hadn't actually mentioned marriage, Hermux couldn't help thinking about it now. It made him very uncomfortable. And what was the deal with Birch and the police, anyway? Did Mirrin even know about that?

Mirrin looked like she was going to faint.

'What is it? Tell me!'

'Hermux, this is very difficult for me. I don't know who you talked to. But it wasn't Birch! Birch and I didn't break up. Birch is dead! He died years ago!'

Chapter 16
OLD MONEY TALKS

'Tucka?' Skimpy purred. 'Why don't you join us?'

Elusa and Birkanny waved and motioned her towards the table.

'We were just talking about you ...'

Tucka smiled tentatively. She loved to be talked about.

'It's so embarrassing, but none of us can remember exactly how your great-great-grandparents made their fortune. Isn't that silly? It's completely slipped our minds.'

The question took Tucka by surprise.

'My great-great-grandparents? Goodness! You know, I don't really know very much about them. Probably pretty ordinary people.'

Skimpy nudged Birkanny's foot with a delicate tap.

'Then it was your great-grandparents that made all the money?' asked Birkanny with a lovely questioning gesture.

'Oh, heavens, no!' Tucka laughed. 'They were farmers. And that was a step up for them!'

Elusa laid her paw encouragingly on Tucka's arm.

'That's marvellous! Farmers! Tillers of the soil! So it fell on the shoulders of your grandparents to make the family fortune? Who would have imagined?'

'Oh, no! It wasn't them. Not by a long shot! My mother's father was a shoemaker. My father's parents ran a little grocery shop. A sweet little place. I remember playing there as a little girl. Grandmother Mertslin was a wonderful, wonderful cook. I remember her baking ...'

At that moment Hinkum Stepfitchler III sauntered past them, nibbling delicately on a Gorgonzola cheese puff. Skimpy reached for his arm and pulled him into the group.

'Hinkum dear! You've got to hear this. It's positively fascinating. Tucka's great-grandparents didn't have a dime. And her grandparents were nobodies. Absolute nobodies. Her grandmother was a cook!'

'She wasn't a *cook*,' Tucka tried to explain to Hinkum.

'I don't suppose your grandmother is looking for work,' interrupted Elusa. 'My cook is a temperamental little shrew. I'd fire her in a minute if I could replace her.'

'My grandmother was NOT a cook!' sputtered Tucka. 'I said she was a wonderful cook. She used to bake me the most wonderful biscuits shaped like little –'

'So it was your parents who made the Mertslin money!' Skimpy announced with enormous satisfaction. 'Imagine it! Your own mother and father slaving away with their bare paws. It's like an old fairy tale.'

'You poor, wretched creature!' Birkanny joined in. 'You must have seen them working with your own eyes. Crying in the arms of your nanny as Mama and Papa marched off to work every day. Shovels in hand or whatever they used to earn their meagre daily bread. How pitiful! What on earth could that have been like for you? So depressing!'

'It's a miracle you weren't permanently affected,' Elusa joined in. 'Deprived! Blighted! Stunted beyond hope! You must tell us absolutely everything about your dreary childhood. Spare us no detail, no matter how painful. And tell us, how did your poor, pathetic parents finally make the family fortune? Some trick of fate? We're all simply dying to know.'

'Well, actually, it wasn't my parents who made the Mertslin millions,' Tucka admitted.

'Oh! Now I see it!' Skimpy declared. 'A freak inheritance!'

'No,' said Tucka simply. 'I made it.'

'You?' said Skimpy, suppressing a giggle. 'Whatever do you mean?'

'I mean that I made it,' said Tucka. She lifted her chin and looked Skimpy straight in the eye. 'The Mertslin money! I made every single penny of it. Myself. Me. Tucka Mertslin! The Queen of Beauty!'

'Oh, my dear Tucka!' Skimpy grasped Elusa's hand in shock. 'I'm so terribly sorry. I had no idea.' Elusa winked at Birkanny, who winked back. Skimpy winked at Hinkum. But he didn't see her. His eyes were entirely on Tucka.

'What an utterly charming story,' Hinkum drawled. 'It is so seldom that one meets someone of such vitality, intelligence and determination. How delightful to discover that such achievement is still possible in today's world.'

He bowed deeply.

'And that such excellence of character,' he continued, 'should be so exquisitely packaged.'

Tucka said a small prayer of thanks that at that very moment the tantalizing aroma of fresh popcorn wafted from the buffet table and brought the flies on her dress back to life. Tucka was enveloped in a rainbow of dancing colour.

'Packaging has always been my passion,' said Tucka with a dreamy look in her eyes.

Chapter 17
SONG AND DANCE

As the mournful cry of accordions announced the beginning of a slow tango, Tucka and Hinkum found themselves irresistibly drawn towards the dance floor.

Hinkum placed his hand at the small of Tucka's back, just above her tightly cinched waist. Ignoring the tickle of whirring wings, he guided her into the crowd with the easy confidence of an experienced captain taking the helm of a racing yacht.

'Just how much money would you say you've made so far?' he teased her.

Tucka looked up at him through a rose-tinted fog. 'More than I could ever possibly spend by myself,' she murmured.

Hinkum pulled her close, pivoted suddenly, reversed direction and dipped.

Tucka burst into laughter.

'Oh, you are a naughty mouse! Aren't you?'

The red gleam in his eye was all the answer she needed.

The tango gave way to a zesty shimmy-hop with a pounding beat.

Tucka broke away from Hinkum.

'Let's be bad!' she squealed.

Hinkum hopped straight into the air.

Tucka gave a violent shake to the left. Hinkum jumped to the right. Tucka flutter-twisted forward. Hinkum bounded backwards. Tucka did a whirling wigwag. Hinkum did a flying hopscotch. Tucka shivered. Hinkum skipped. Tucka twitched.

And that was her mistake.

Tucka's Shoo-Fly Fashion Glue had been carefully tested. It had been submitted to gruelling shakes, to punishing flutter-twists, wild wigwags and shattering shivers. But it had never been twitched.

Ten thousand flies suddenly found themselves catapulted through space and free to land where they chose.

They chose quickly.

They chose plates and spoons and bowls and glasses. They landed on lips. They flew up nostrils. They crawled around ears. And wherever they went, they nibbled and buzzed. It was the most fun they had ever had.

But it wouldn't last long.

The party was over.

Chapter 18
BED OF ROSES

Terfle dreamed that she and Hermux were visiting a greenhouse. Rows and rows of roses stretched in every direction. Hermux lifted her high into the air on his paw and released her. She extended her wings and flew away. Exhilarated by the sweet fragrance that hung in the air, she soon lost sight of him. A sprawling tea rose caught her eye. When she descended to investigate, she found herself in a great forest of stems looking up into a glowing canopy of pink and green buds. Each bud was sugared to its very tip with plump, sticky aphids.

Terfle's mouth watered as she began the long, long climb up a thorny stem. As hard as she tried, she could not move faster than a snail's pace. And a slow snail at that. After what seemed like hours and hours she finally reached the first bud. But before she could taste a single aphid, the sound of a key grating in a lock sent her into a sudden panic. They were locking up the greenhouse for the night. Hermux was going home without her.

Terfle woke up in terror and struggled to her feet. It was well after midnight. Hermux was just getting home from Mirrin's opening. She clambered down from her perch and crawled groggily to the water bowl.

She needed a drink.

Chapter 19
INSTANT REPLAY

Hermux paced up and down in front of Terfle's cage. He was much too excited to even think about going to bed.

'And then Birch and I tackled him and turned him over to the police. Of course, it was actually Birch that tackled him, not me, but it wasn't really Birch, because the real Birch was killed years and years ago, and I was the one that turned him over to the police because Birch disappeared as soon as we even mentioned the police. So the police must be looking for him, although he seems like a very straightforward sort to me. And then I talked to Linka. She was with Dandiffer, who's not nearly so nice as we thought. In fact, I'd like to punch him right in the nose like that rat punched the bad mouse. And she says she's going to sell her aeroplane. Isn't that awful?'

Hermux crossed to his desk and got the little framed photograph of Linka Perflinger and her aeroplane so Terfle could see for herself.

'I can't imagine Linka without her plane,' he said, gazing at the picture. 'It just isn't right.'

Terfle nodded her head gravely.

'Then Linka left, and the next thing I knew, Mirrin was cry-

ing. And Birch is an impostor. And then there are flies everywhere and we had to get out of there in a hurry. Oh! And Linka
kissed me!'

He pointed proudly.

'She kissed me right here on the cheek!'

Terfle stifled a yawn.

'Oh! It's awfully late, isn't it?' Hermux apologized. 'Let's
turn in.'

Hermux undressed and hung up his clothes. He put on his
new winter pyjamas. They were dark blue flannel covered with
silvery white snowflakes.

He washed his face and brushed his teeth and his fur.

Then he plumped up his pillows and crawled into bed. He
opened his journal, uncapped his pen and thought for a moment.
He hardly knew where to begin.

Thank you for puzzles. And for missing pieces. Thank you for
bossy mayors. And silly gossips. Thank you for museums and
painters. And chipmunks. Regardless of who they really are.

Hermux put down his pen and sat quietly for a moment. He
was thinking about his friend Pup Schoonagliffen. Pup had been
the star reporter at the *Daily Sentinel*. He was an expert on everything. But the same adventure that had introduced Hermux to
Linka and restored Mirrin's eyesight had cost Pup his life. Hermux wrote again.

It's on nights like tonight that I find myself really missing Pup.
He would have known just what to say about the whole
evening. He would have found out all about Tucka's dress. And
Dandiffer's expedition. He would have asked the angry mouse

all the right questions. He would have found out what Linka really thought about giving up her plane. And he would have explained the meaning of Mirrin's paintings so all of us could understand.

What a shame to have lost him! In hindsight, I really didn't know Pup at all.

I wonder if we can ever know who people actually are deep down inside. Sometimes people just aren't what they seem to be. Pup seemed like my true friend. It turned out that he wasn't, but I still miss him just the same.

Hermux closed his journal. He switched off the light. He closed his eyes even though he was sure he wouldn't sleep a wink that night.

He was wrong.

He slept like a log.

Chapter 20
POOR SERVICE

Along with the coffee there was a fierce argument brewing at Lanayda's the next morning.

And Hermux walked right into it.

'Hermux, have you seen the paper yet?' Quendle Tiptorf held up the front page of the *Daily Sentinel*.

CAT FIGHT!

Below the headline was a grainy photo of a mob storming the museum steps. Just ahead of the mob ran two scared figures. One of them was dressed like a clown. It was him. Hermux winced. He sat down at his usual place at the counter and smiled sheepishly at Lanayda. She ignored him.

'So?' demanded Quendle. 'Was the party better inside or outside the museum?'

'That's a tough question,' said Hermux, rubbing his head. 'I've never been to a riot before. But I've never been to a museum opening either.'

Hermux waved his fingers at Lanayda. She still hadn't taken his order.

'Lanayda,' Hermux said pleasantly, 'I'll just have the usual.'

'Refresh my memory,' Lanayda replied frostily.

'You know ... the same thing I've had every morning for the last ten years,' Hermux said in surprise. Lanayda stared at him blankly.

'A regular coffee. And a doughnut,' he said very politely. 'What's fresh?'

'They're all fresh!' snapped Lanayda.

'Oh! Sure!' Hermux said. 'Well then, I'll have a cinnamon-sugar cake.'

'Lanayda was just telling us that the REAL party wasn't inside the museum at all. That was just a doddering bunch of old stuffed shirts,' explained Quendle. 'She says that the smart set just stayed for the riot and then went down to the Gopher Hole to see the Growligators. The party there went on until dawn.'

'Oh,' said Hermux.

Lanayda turned away with an exaggerated yawn.

'I said that I'd rather be inside the museum with the food,' Quendle continued. 'What did you get to eat? Was there any corn pudding?'

Before Hermux could answer, the door opened with a merry jingle and in marched Lista Blenwipple.

'Mail!' she announced cheerfully. 'And here, Lanayda, here's that envelope you were looking for last week. From the museum.'

She tossed the useless invitation on to the counter.

'Look at that, would you! It got routed all the way to Couver and back by mistake,' said Lista in disgust. 'There's no excuse for that! This time you really should file a complaint.'

Chapter 21
IDENTITY CRISIS

The old chipmunk was waiting at the shop door when Hermux returned.

'The sign here says you'll be back in ten minutes,' he complained. 'I've been waiting for twenty at least.'

'Approximately ten minutes. That's what the sign means,' Hermux replied as he unlocked the shop. He was in no mood to be lectured.

'Then it should say "approximately ten minutes". Say what you mean, boy. Don't beat around the bush!'

'You're one to talk about beating around the bush!' Hermux said irritably. 'How about saying what you mean for a change? Who are you really? And what do you want?'

'I told you, I'm Birch Tentintrotter.'

'Right. And Mirrin told me that Birch Tentintrotter is dead! He died years ago.'

'You told Mirrin you spoke to me?'

'Of course I did! Why wouldn't I?'

'I thought you would wait until you and I talked ... until I explained –'

'You and I *did* speak. Last night. At the museum. Remember?' Hermux eyed his visitor warily. Maybe the old guy wasn't all there.

'Oh, no!' said the old chipmunk. 'How did she take it?'

'How did she take it? How do you think she took it? She was miserable! And furious! At me. For even mentioning your name. Or his name. Who are you, anyway?'

'I'm Birch. Really I am. Everyone thinks I'm dead. They think I died in a boat wreck on the Longish River. Forty years ago. That's what they reported in the papers. My body was never found. It was easier and better all around for me to just disappear.'

'So you just left Mirrin in the lurch? Left her broken-hearted all these years, thinking you were dead? Boy, that's true love if I ever heard it!'

'You don't understand!'

'Of course I don't understand!' Hermux fumed. 'How on earth could I understand? You haven't told me anything but your name. And even that's questionable!'

'You're right. You're right. But it's a long story. I'd better begin at the beginning.'

Chapter 22
BY THE BOOK

'It was so long ago that sometimes it seems like it was only a dream,' the old chipmunk began. 'I came to Pinchester to study at Stepfitchler University. I majored in ancient languages with a speciality in Old Mouse.'

He sipped from the cup of tea that Hermux had made for him.

'Mirrin and I and your mother and father met in our freshman year and quickly became good friends. It was an exciting time at the university and a very happy time for us. When we graduated, your father and mother married, and your father went to work here at your grandfather's shop. Mirrin went to the Museum School to study painting. And I stayed on at the university. I was the first chipmunk to be admitted to the doctoral studies programme in Old Mouse. Naturally, there was a lot of pressure on me to perform. And I performed well. I was bright. I worked hard. And I loved the work. I loved the old library. I loved handling the old books. I loved translating the old texts. And I loved Mirrin. We never meant to fall in love. In fact, we tried not to. We knew it wouldn't be easy for us. Even at the university, people made comments. And outside it was impossible.

My family didn't trust Mirrin. Her family hated me. But despite all that, it seemed like it might work out. At least for a while. At the end of my first year, Professor Stepfitchler chose me to be his research and teaching assistant.'

'But he seems so young!' said Hermux.

'No, it wasn't Hinkum. Hinkum was only a boy then. It was Hinkum's father, the great Professor Stervin Stepfitchler. The world's foremost authority on Old Mouse. He was just beginning to work on his translation of *The Book of Peas*. And I was his protégé. It was an enormous honour. He was grooming me for a professorship. Imagine how I felt! The first chipmunk professor of Old Mouse. I proposed to Mirrin then, and she accepted. We had a bright future ahead of us. I had my own office on campus. I had my own classes to teach. I was even given my own keys to the Rare Books Library. And that's when the trouble began.'

Birch paused a moment.

'The Rare Books Library,' he continued dreamily. 'The original Stepfitchler Collection. For someone in my field it was the centre of the universe. I practically lived there. If I wasn't teaching or with Mirrin, I was at the library. One night I was there alone working very late. I was sitting at a table in the main reading room, and I must have dozed off. A crash woke me. An old atlas had fallen from one of the bookcases. When I went to replace it, I found a map that had slipped from its pages. It was old, much older than the atlas, and it was covered with the most curious symbols. Not like anything I'd ever seen before, even in the oldest Old Mouse scrolls. It was incredibly exciting. And in my excitement I made a terrible mistake.'

Chapter 23

MIDNIGHT OIL

'I kept it a secret! I should have turned the map over to the library. I should have reported it immediately. But I was blinded by greed. If it was the chance of a lifetime, I wanted it all for myself.'

'What did you do?' asked Hermux.

'I sneaked the map out of the library, and for the next month I worked on translating it secretly at night in my office. I didn't even mention it to Mirrin until I thought I had cracked the code.'

'What did it say?'

'It wasn't what it said that seemed important. It was how it said it.'

'How?'

'The map was notated in hieroglyphic symbols. It was a completely unknown language. I searched the library for any mention of it anywhere. Even the tiniest fragment on a broken piece of pottery. But there was no record.'

'Maybe it was a fake?'

'That was what I thought too. So I took a sample of the paper and had the chemistry department analyse it. That was very tricky. Their tests showed that it was more than three thousand years old. But that was impossible. They wanted to know where I had found it. I told them that Mirrin and some of her friends at the museum had doctored up a piece of old papyrus as a practical joke on one their professors.'

'So it was really old!'

'I thought it was. I thought it was the genuine article. And if I could translate it, it would completely change our understanding of ancient history. It would mean that Old Mouse was not the first written language after all. It would mean that some sort of civilization came before ours. Maybe mice were not the first creatures to read and write, after all.'

'I see,' said Hermux thoughtfully. And he did. For the very first time. 'That would put things in a very different light, wouldn't it?'

'Exactly. And I thought I was the chipmunk to do it. It was the sort of thing that ambitious young scholars dream about.' He stopped and looked at Hermux with great seriousness. 'It was also the sort of thing that could make a young chipmunk lose sight of what really mattered to him.'

'So, what did it say?' demanded Hermux. 'Did you translate it?'

'I did. Or I thought I did. It was even more peculiar than I thought.'

'How?'

'According to my translation of the symbols, it was the map to a royal library hidden in the desert.'

'But how could there be a library if there weren't any books yet?'

'Well, apparently there were.'

'But where are they, then?'

'Lost, destroyed, or still hidden. There is no way of knowing.'

'Then find the library!' insisted Hermux.

'That's what I set out to do. But there is one more thing I haven't mentioned. The map was written in Cat. The library, if it really ever existed, was the royal library of a kingdom of cats.'

'How do you know?'

'Well, actually I don't know. It was my theory. My theory of cats. And I can tell you that it wasn't well received at Stepfitchler University. Or in Pinchester for that matter. That's why I had to leave town and disappear.'

Chapter 24
CLASSIFIED

'Well, what's the theory?' Hermux demanded.

'The key to the hieroglyphs was a figure seated on a throne. But it wasn't like anything any of us have ever seen. At least until last night ...'

'You mean it looked like one of Mirrin's creatures?'

'Very close. It had a large head. A flattish face. Great fanged teeth. Hooked claws on each paw. Those peculiar slitted eyes. And it was enormous. Much larger than a mouse. Or a chipmunk. Or a squirrel.'

'And this was the king?'

'Apparently.'

'What did it say?'

'Word for word?'

'If you remember.'

'I'll never forget it. All right. Here goes.' Birch closed his eyes and began in a singsong voice to recite.

'"Librarian and scribe needed to manage extensive library. Sunny year-round climate. Comfortable living quarters. Excellent benefits. Experienced only. Mechanical skills a plus. Apply in person." Then there was a sketchy little map showing the location.'

'It's just a want ad!'

'I know. I was surprised too. But that's what it said. Believe me, I worked on it around the clock.'

'But what about the cat king?'

'It was signed with a royal seal and a list of the king's names: Ka-Narsh-Pah, Eye-of-Heaven, Talon-of-Justice, Strength-of-Many, Merciful-Paw, Father-of-All.'

'You left town and deserted Mirrin over a want ad for a cat king's library?' Hermux asked incredulously. 'I hate to say this, Birch, because you seem like a nice guy, but you're nuts!'

'That's exactly what Professor Stepfitchler said. Sometimes I think he was right.'

'So, what happened?'

'I started researching cat mythology. Mirrin helped me. But we couldn't find anything. There is nothing written about our belief in cats except for a few snatches of children's rhymes. Then I went to the Rare Books Library and asked the reference librarian for help. That very afternoon I was called into Professor Stepfitchler's office. He wanted to know all about my sudden interest in cats. Maybe I should have told him about the map right then. But I didn't. "Just curiosity," I told him. "Curiosity has killed many scholarly careers," he warned me. "I'd give it up if I were you." But I didn't. The possibility of a cat kingdom three thousand years ago with a civilization advanced enough to have libraries would completely rewrite our notion of history. And the person that proved it would have a prominent place in all the history that followed.'

'What did you do?'

'I wrote up my findings in a paper. With the translation and the map. I presented it to the university and requested funding to mount an expedition to search for the library.'

'And?'

'I was fired. They padlocked my office and ordered me off the campus.'

Chapter 25
PUBLISH OR PERISH

'So you left?' Hermux asked.

'No. I fought it.'

'How?'

'I published the paper myself. We printed it right here in your shop. In this very room. I found an old, broken printing press. Your father got it running. Your mother set the type. Mirrin ran the press. We were going to distribute the paper on campus and demand my reinstatement on grounds of academic freedom. We managed to print a hundred copies before the police shut us down. They arrested all of us, confiscated the press and the papers, and closed your grandfather's shop.'

'For publishing a paper about cats?'

'Not exactly,' Birch explained. 'We were charged with theft and possession of stolen property.'

Hermux stared at him in disbelief.

'The map. It belonged to the library. I had taken it without permission.'

'I'm starting to remember this,' said Hermux grimly. 'You're the one my grandfather called Mr Troublemaker. Whenever he was mad at my father, he called him Mr Big Shot. "Leave it to

Mr Big Shot and Mr Troublemaker. They know what's best for all of us. If it were up to the two of you, we'd be starving now!" I can still hear him! No wonder Dad never mentioned you. You nearly lost his father's shop and got him thrown out of the house!'

'I warned you that I was trouble, Hermux.'

'Yeah, but I thought you were kidding.'

'I wasn't.'

'Then what happened?'

'The university agreed to drop the charges if I returned the map and surrendered all of my notes.'

'And?'

'I did it. What choice did I have? I never meant to get everyone into trouble. Certainly not into trouble with the law. But that wasn't the end of it.'

'What else could they do?'

'I never found out who it was. But I started getting telephone calls. Late at night. At first no one was there. Just silence. Then a horrible, chilling voice. "Here, kitty, kitty, kitty! Here, kitty, kitty, kitty!" Over and over. And then an awful shrieking laugh. I thought I was losing my mind. Then the ticket came in the mail.'

'The ticket?'

'A train ticket. With a note. It told me to leave Pinchester that day. "Or your cute little artist friend won't look so good! If she's ever seen again! Ha! Ha!" I left on the six o'clock Northbound. And I've never been back until now.'

'You've been dead until now.'

'Right. I keep forgetting. Whoever wanted me out of Pinchester apparently thought Twyrp was far enough away to keep me out of mischief. That's as far as the ticket took me. I had a strange feeling that I was being followed. So I –'

'Wait a minute!' Hermux broke in. 'Did you ever tell Mirrin about the calls and the ticket?'

'No, I thought she would be safer.'

'So you just disappeared?'

Birch nodded his head sadly.

'Well, it's time you explained it to her,' said Hermux. 'All these years she's thought you were dead. And if you're not dead, she deserves to know why.'

Birch looked at him oddly.

'You know what I mean,' Hermux said. 'You owe her an explanation. And believe me, it had better be a good one!'

Chapter 26
SURPRISE!

It wasn't until he knocked that Hermux had second thoughts. Maybe surprising Mirrin like this wasn't such a good idea after all. She was in for a shock. But at least it was a good one. Or so he hoped. Right now he was more worried about Birch, who looked like he couldn't decide whether to faint or run away.

Hermux gripped him firmly by the paw as Mirrin opened the door.

'Hermux?' Mirrin asked, peering at him over her reading glasses. 'I was just getting ready to start lunch. Was I expecting you?'

'No,' Hermux began. 'It's kind of a surprise.'

'Well, come in!' Mirrin opened the door wider and saw Birch. The welcoming smile faded from her face.

She stepped very close to Birch and looked up into his face. 'Who are you?' she demanded, adjusting her glasses to see him more clearly.

Birch just stood there speechless.

'It's Birch,' explained Hermux.

'Birch?' Mirrin repeated. 'But Birch is dead. Birch was

killed in a boat wreck. On the Longish River. I still have the newspaper clipping.'

Hermux nodded to Birch.

'Say something!' he told him.

Birch opened his mouth, but nothing came out. A tear rolled down his cheek.

'It's really him,' Hermux reassured her. 'At least I think it is.'

Mirrin took one of Birch's trembling paws in hers and sniffed it carefully. She turned it over and smelled the inside of his wrist. She stared hard at Birch.

'Birch!' she wailed and wrapped her arms around him fiercely.

'Mirrin!' Birch answered in a choked voice. He nuzzled her delicate ears.

'You're alive! You're alive! I can't believe it!' Mirrin alternated between laughing and crying. 'You came back! You came back to me!'

After a few minutes she disengaged herself from the embrace and stepped back. Without any warning she slapped Birch right across the face.

'Where have you been?' she cried, pounding his chest with her fists. 'How could you leave me like that? How could you let me suffer like that? Alone. My whole life! How could you do it?'

'Mirrin!' Hermux yelled, pulling her away from Birch. 'Stop it! You'll hurt him!'

Birch stood rubbing his cheek. Mirrin struggled to catch her breath.

'No, Hermux,' Birch said. 'Mirrin is right. I deserve it. I deserve much more than that.'

Mirrin wiped her eyes with a handkerchief. 'I don't know what came over me,' she apologized. She offered Birch her paw somewhat formally. 'Thank goodness you're alive, Birch,' she said simply. 'It's good to see you! Goodness, why are we all standing here outside? Come in! Come in! I'll make some tea.' Then she turned and hurried away down the hall towards the kitchen.

Birch and Hermux gaped at each other in confusion.

'I don't know what I expected,' Birch sighed. He looked very old and very tired.

Chapter 27
UNANSWERED QUESTIONS

Despite the cheerful fire in the fireplace, Mirrin's living room seemed cold and cheerless. Hermux and Birch waited miserably on the couch for Mirrin to emerge from the kitchen.

Finally Hermux rose and stood before the fire. He made a great show of warming his hands. Then he turned and studied the painting that hung above the mantel as though it was new to him. It was a dark image of broken rocks and tangled tree roots. Hermux had always found it curiously soothing.

'You've never really seen much of Mirrin's work, have you?' Hermux asked. 'Except for the cats?'

Birch didn't answer.

'I think I'll see if Mirrin needs help in the kitchen,' said Hermux. He left Birch staring gloomily into the fire.

In the kitchen, Hermux found Mirrin sitting at the table with her face buried in her paws. A tray was partially set with cups and saucers. A teapot sat ready on the counter. The tea-kettle whistled angrily on the stove.

'What are you doing in here?' Hermux hissed.

Mirrin looked up at him reluctantly. Her eyes were red from crying.

'I can't go in there, Hermux,' she sobbed. 'I can't face him. I made a fool of myself out there. Shouting at him, "You've come back to me! You've come back to me!" He's probably married. A nice little chipmunk wife. With grandchildren. And what do I have? What was I waiting for all these years? Why did he come back? Why did he come back now? Why now?'

Hermux turned off the kettle and filled the teapot.

'I don't know,' Hermux admitted, feeling very stupid. 'I keep intending to find out. But I keep forgetting to ask.'

'Well?' Mirrin asked impatiently.

'Well what?'

'Tell me!'

'Tell you what?'

'Is he married?'

'No, he's not married!' Hermux said impatiently. 'Of course not! At least I don't think he is. He hasn't mentioned anything about being married.'

'Hermux!' Mirrin implored.

'Well, let's get this cleared up right now. Let's go ask him.'

'I don't want to ask him.'

'I'll ask him.'

'I don't want you to!'

'Well then, what do you want?'

'I just want to know. That's all.'

'All right then. We'll find out. Subtly. Leave it to me.'

Chapter 28
DIPLOMATIC ENQUIRY

Hermux carried the tea tray into the living room and set it carefully on the low glass table. Birch stood by the fire, gazing up intently at Mirrin's painting.

'She's a very powerful painter, isn't she?' said Birch. 'Look at this. It makes you want to just walk away from everything. Just leave it behind. Go back to the forest and find a simpler way to live. Mirrin always saw the world more clearly than the rest of us.'

'She still does,' said Hermux. 'But she's a fighter. She refuses to walk away from it.'

'Birch, I hope you still like crispy grubs!' Mirrin called from the doorway.

'With salty vinegar?' he answered eagerly.

'Of course! And spicy crumbs.'

Mirrin brought in an enormous bowl of grubs, plus the dips, a big cheese board, and a basket of nutty crackers. She poured tea for each of them.

'Do you still take milk?' she asked Birch. Their eyes met for an instant, curious and hopeful.

He nodded and smiled. The warm fragrance of the tea filled

the room. And for a moment they were content to sit together and listen to the reassuring crackle of the fire.

Hermux cleared his throat. 'Birch,' he said uncomfortably. 'I'm still puzzled by a few things.'

'Yes?'

'Well, you've never said why you've come back just now. And that's very curious. I thought there was a mystery of some sort. And you've never said what it is. But before we get to any of that, Mirrin needs to know whether or not you're married.'

Mirrin let out a howl and covered her face in embarrassment. Hermux ducked instinctively. And Birch rose clumsily to his feet.

Then he dropped to his knees before Mirrin and very gently took one of her paws in his.

'Mirrin,' he began. 'You are the only love of my life. I have never so much as looked at another woman. I never dared to let myself imagine this moment. Seeing you again. Thinking that you would even remember me. Much less care about me one way or the other.'

Mirrin ran her paw gently across the scar of Birch's missing ear.

'I need to know what happened, Birch,' she told him seriously. 'I need to understand who you are and why you left. And where you've been. And why you've come back.'

'Tell her, Birch!' said Hermux through a mouthful of nutty crackers. The tension in the room had made him incredibly hungry. 'Start with the phone calls.'

'What phone calls?' asked Mirrin.

'It was just after all of you got out of jail,' Hermux told her. 'After you printed the cat paper. Birch started getting threatening phone calls late at night.'

'But why didn't you tell me, Birch?' Mirrin demanded sternly. 'Who was it? What did they say?'

'Tell her the whole thing,' Hermux encouraged.

'I don't know who it was. At first I thought it was a joke. A weird voice. "Here, kitty, kitty! Here, kitty, kitty!" And a weirder laugh. But it wasn't funny. It was frightening. I thought it would stop eventually. Then I got a train ticket in the mail. And a note that said you would get hurt badly if I didn't leave Pinchester immediately.'

'And so you just left without telling me anything?' Mirrin asked in disbelief.

'I was frightened for you. I knew you wouldn't want me to leave. I was trying to protect you. I didn't want you to get hurt.'

'But I did get hurt!' she said angrily. 'Don't you understand?'

'I do now,' Birch said.

'Then why didn't you come back? Why did you let us think you were dead?'

'When I got to Twyrp, I thought things would blow over. I thought that whoever it was would forget about me. And after a few weeks I could come back. But someone followed me there. Things started happening. My notebook was stolen out of my room. I was pushed off a crowded pavement in front of a truck and barely escaped getting run over. I decided it was time to move on. I knew that finding the library was my only real chance to get my life back. So I decided to look for it. The problem was, I had no idea where to begin. The map had only been a detail. Where did it fit in? The Great Desert was my hunch. Most of it is still unexplored. And the desert offered the best chance for any trace of a library to survive for three thousand years. So I slipped out of town on foot and headed west to the Longish River. When

I got there, I caught a ride on a barge heading upstream. I was sure I had escaped. The first night out on the river I bedded down on the deck and went to sleep. Nothing seemed out of the ordinary. It must have been three in the morning when I woke up with the most horrible pain in my head. My arms were held to my sides. Someone was sitting on my chest, and he was driving a nail through my ear into the deck. I passed out. A splash of cold water woke me up, and I discovered that the barge was sinking.'

Chapter 29
A CUT ABOVE THE REST

'Yikes!' exclaimed Hermux.

'I had to cut off my own ear with my pocketknife.'

'Oh, Birch! How horrible!' said Mirrin. She reached over and tenderly stroked the scar on Birch's head.

'That had to hurt!' Hermux unconsciously rubbed his own ear. Birch didn't look so clownish to him now.

'I suppose it did. I was so panicked that I didn't really feel it. Or rather, I really felt it badly. But I didn't have time to think about it. I was swimming for my life. I made it to shore and hid there in the reeds until it was light.'

'But why would someone want to kill you? And why did they go to so much trouble? What were they afraid of?'

'I don't know. We all knew that the subject of cats was controversial. I assumed it was because I was a chipmunk, and I was tampering with mouse history. That I had crossed a line that somebody in Pinchester wouldn't stand for. And I was being taught a lesson.'

'There's something more to it than that,' said Mirrin. 'I just feel it. There's something very odd here.'

'All I knew was that they really meant business. I laid low and followed the river. It was days until I came to a town. I was half starved. And half crazy from the heat and the sun. I was on the front page of the first newspaper I saw:

FUGITIVE CHIPMUNK DROWNS IN FREAK SHIPPING ACCIDENT

'At first I wanted to tell everyone I wasn't dead. Then I thought about it. Being dead meant there was no more reason to kill me. And no more reason to threaten you. So I stayed dead. It seemed better for everybody concerned. I didn't think it would be for very long. But one by one the years slipped away. One day I woke up and realized that it was too late for me to come back to life. I had nothing to show for the time I'd wasted. And no one to show it to.'

'But what about Mirrin?' Hermux wanted to know, pointedly.

Birch frowned. He looked down at his worn paws.

'I thought I was doing the best thing for you,' he told Mirrin in a choked voice. 'I thought it was better for you to start over. With someone of your own kind. With someone who didn't ruin everything he touched.'

Mirrin sat quietly thinking.

'I did start over,' she said finally, with some bitterness. 'By myself. And that's the life I've lived.'

Hermux held his breath. Birch's ear twitched uncomfortably.

'I've never found anyone of my own kind,' Mirrin continued. 'Except you, Birch.'

Hermux got clumsily to his feet.

'I'm going to put some more water on for tea,' he said.

But neither Mirrin nor Birch heard him.

Chapter 30
OFF THE MAP

Hermux stood in the kitchen doorway, listening. It was awfully quiet in the living room. But he couldn't wait any longer. He rattled the lid on the teapot.

'There!' he announced loudly. 'There's nothing like a pot of fresh tea.' He marched in brusquely and set the tea down.

Birch and Mirrin smiled up at him and nodded happily. They sat side by side, hand in hand. They had both been crying, but they looked better for it. The tension was gone out of the room, and in its place there was a wonderful, warm feeling of relief.

'Shall I pour?' asked Mirrin.

Hermux busied himself at the fireplace. He stirred the coals and added a few plump little fir logs to the fire.

'Well, Birch?' Hermux asked, trying to sound calm. 'You escaped from drowning. You found your way to the nearest town. Then what happened?'

'I redrew the map as well as I could from memory. Then I worked my way up and down the river, doing odd jobs for money, and started looking for a canyon with plum-coloured walls.'

'A canyon?'

'The map placed the library at the end of a canyon with its mouth on the bank of a river. The note on the map said, "Watch for a plum-coloured canyon. Hard to miss." My guess was the Longish River. So that's where I started. On foot at first. It was slow and difficult. Weeks stretched into months. I found brown canyons and yellow canyons and orange canyons. Even striped canyons. But not a single one that was plum-coloured. I got a job on a barge so I could learn the river. Then I explored the tributaries and worked my way into the desert. I looked every-where. I asked everyone I met about a plum-coloured canyon. I asked about any legends of ruins or monuments. I followed every lead. But they all turned out to be dead ends. Two years ago I finally gave up.'

'I don't understand,' said Hermux, disappointed. 'I thought you found something.'

'I did. But not until after I had stopped looking. I settled down in a little town and took a job in a shop. A junk shop, if you want to know the truth. The owner had died, and his son hired me to clean the place up. That's what I was doing when I found these.'

Birch retrieved his backpack from the hallway and removed a small cardboard tube and what looked like a gear to a large machine. It had very long, very sharp teeth. One of them was broken off.

Birch handed the tube to Mirrin. 'Open it,' he told her.

He handed the gear to Hermux, who was so surprised by its heaviness that he nearly dropped it.

'This must be bronze!' said Hermux.

'It is,' said Birch. 'It's well over three thousand years old.'

'But that's impossible! This looks like an escape wheel for a

93

giant clock. Clocks were only invented eight hundred years ago, and nobody used bronze.'

'I thought you would be interested.'

'Oh, look, it's a scroll!' exclaimed Mirrin. She slipped a roll of papyrus from the cardboard tube. 'May I open it?'

'Of course,' Birch told her. 'But be careful. It's fragile.'

Chapter 31
THE VOICE OF DOOM

The papyrus was the bleached yellow of September hay. Mirrin unrolled it gently on the coffee table, smoothing its edges carefully. She and Hermux leaned in close and studied the odd marks and symbols that covered the surface.

'What is it?' they both asked.

'I believe it's a message from the librarian and scribe of the Royal Library. Possibly the very one who answered the want ad I found. Look, here is the same royal seal.' He pointed to a rectangular box at the bottom corner of the scroll. Inside the box sat a crowned figure surrounded by smaller pictographs. It looked like one of the creatures in Mirrin's paintings.

Hermux felt a little queasy.

'So your map wasn't a fake,' Mirrin said hopefully. 'You were right all along.'

'I believe I was, and I think this is the proof.'

'But how did it get to the junk shop?'

'I have no idea. People brought things in. It had probably been sitting there for fifty years or more. Someone must have dug it up somewhere in the area and sold it as a curio.'

'Can you tell us what it says?' asked Hermux, although he

wasn't entirely sure that he wanted to know. 'Have you been able to translate it?'

'This first symbol, the eye, is easy. It's a phonogram for the word *I*. Similar to Old Mouse. The second symbol is a little harder. The thought bubble, here, indicates a mental process of some sort. The heart inside it is a modifier. I tried several possibilities and settled on the word *hope*. The third symbol, the mirror, had me stumped me for a long time. And I realized I was trying too hard. What do you see when you look in a mirror?'

'Yourself?' asked Hermux.

'Precisely. The mirror is the word *you*. Simple, isn't it? Verbs turn out to be another thing entirely. They are almost mathematical in a way ...'

Hermux couldn't wait for the full explanation.

'Just read it to us!' he told Birch.

'All right, all right.'

He ran the tip of his paw across the scroll, pointing to each symbol as he read aloud.

☥ I hope that whoever finds this is a friend.
The palace is broken. The temples are in flames.
The city is laid waste. The people are
destroyed. All that we have built is gone. The little
slaves vow they will erase us from the earth.

If you are a friend, be a true one!! Repair the
wheels of time in the Tomb of the King. Restore the
King's Delight and bring Ka-Narsh-Pah back to life.
Perhaps then the kingdom's harmony will be
restored.

If you are a friend, do this.

If you are not a friend, then even hope is gone.
☞ I fear I am the last, and my end is near.

Prowlah Paad
Librarian

'And what are these symbols on the back of the scroll?' asked Mirrin.

'I think it's a shopping list,' said Birch. 'Here's what I think happened. This wheel was part of some sort of time machine that sustained the king in eternal life. It broke. Prowlah the scribe came into the city to get it repaired. Unfortunately, while he was there, the slaves revolted, overthrew the cats and destroyed their kingdom and everything in it. Prowlah was trapped somewhere. He wrote this letter on the back of the shopping list and hid it, with the wheel, in a place where he thought it would be safe. And it was, for almost three thousand years, until someone found it and thought it was a piece of junk to sell.'

'But who were the slaves?' asked Hermux.

'They may have been mice,' said Birch.

'Not very likely!' Hermux retorted. 'Mice are much too proud and independent to be enslaved. And the idea that we would destroy things is very far-fetched. Mice are builders, not destroyers. And even if it's true, then why haven't we ever found any evidence before this?'

'Mice can be destructive when they wish,' said Birch ruefully. 'And they can be very vindictive.'

'As odd as it all sounds, there's something about this that has a peculiar ring of truth to it,' said Mirrin. 'And besides,

97

Hermux, Birch is right. Mice can be very vindictive. I found this in my mailbox this morning.'

She took an envelope down from the mantel and handed it to Hermux. It was crudely addressed to 'The Mouse Traitor'. Inside was a scrawled note:

Dear miss fancy Artist,

when are you going to learn who your people are? Maybe mice were better off when you were blind. Maybe that can be arranged. And maybe this time it will be for good.

think it over.
the Brotherhood of Mice

'Well, it's not very brotherly, is it?' said Hermux.

Birch tore the letter from Hermux's paw. He read it quickly and then struggled to his feet.

'That's it!' he said, reaching for the scroll. 'I'm destroying all of this. I'm not taking any more chances. I'm done with it.'

Mirrin stood at the fire, gazing into it. She turned slowly and spoke in a very calm, but firm, voice. 'Birch, put the scroll back and sit down. You're not destroying anything. This cat thing has nearly destroyed both of us. But that's finished. We've seen it through this far, and now we're going to see it through to the end. We're going to find this library. And we're going to discover once and for all if cats actually existed or if this has just been a horrible hoax. We're going to do it whether we like the answer or not.'

Birch tried to interrupt, but Mirrin went on.

'We're going to find out who has been threatening us and why. We're going to put a stop to it. And we're going to pick up our lives again and live them as well as we can for the time we've got left.'

She took a deep breath.

'Now tell us, Birch, why did you come back? What were you thinking? What did you want? What is your plan?'

Chapter 32
MEMORY LANE

The towering bronze statue of Kernel Stepfitchler stared down accusingly at Hermux and Birch as they made their way through the massive stone entrance gate of Stepfitchler University.

'I hope we're not late,' Hermux told Birch. 'Mirrin said seven o'clock sharp.' He opened his silver peapod pocket watch and examined it in the flickering gaslight. 'We've got five minutes. Do you remember how to get there?'

'I think I could find it blindfolded,' Birch said.

'Good. Because it couldn't get much darker. What do you think he'll say?'

'I don't know. He'll want to examine the scroll and quiz me about the translation. Then he'll report to the museum board. And they'll make a decision about the expedition. Who is Ortolina Perriflot, anyway? And what does she have to do with it?'

'Ortolina Perriflot is the richest woman in the world. She's the head of the Perriflot Institute and a very old friend of Mirrin's. She set up the meeting with Stepfitchler. According to Mirrin, if he supports us, the board will go along. And if he opposes us, it's going to be a tough sell.'

They reached a fork in the walkway and Birch hesitated. 'We turn right here,' he said after a moment. 'Then we'll turn left, go through a grove of birch trees, over a little bridge and then up the hill to the Stepfitchler Mansion.'

It was exactly the way Birch remembered it, except for the tall iron security fence that surrounded the mansion. 'This is new,' he said. 'How do you suppose we get in?'

Hermux felt around in the dark and found the buzzer beside the gate. A minute later a sombre voice enquired, 'Yes?'

Hermux wasn't sure where to speak. 'Hermux Tantamoq and Professor Birch Tentintrotter to see Dr Stepfitchler!' he said at the top of his voice.

'One moment.'

Quite a few moments later, the voice returned. 'Please come in, Dr Stepfitchler is expecting you.'

There was a faint click and then silence. Birch pushed against the gate and it swung open slowly. A faint light came on, barely illuminating the outlines of a broad flight of stairs that rose steeply ahead of them.

As they started the climb, Birch cautioned Hermux. 'Go easy on the "professor" business. It's a touchy subject around here.' He turned and pointed below them. 'Look, Hermux! Down there. It's the Rare Books Library. Just there through those trees. You can see right into it from here. That's the map room where I was working. Gosh, this is really giving me the creeps. The great Professor Stepfitchler's only son. This whole thing is going to be very touchy.'

'Take it easy, Birch. That was a long time ago. Ortolina set this up, and she says that Hinkum is very interested. Besides, what does he have to lose? He's Hinkum Stepfitchler the Third.

Practically the most famous person in the world. Or at least the most famous name. He's even got his own university. No offence, but I can't see you and your cats being much of a threat to him.'

Chapter 33
THE MARCH OF HISTORY

'The master will join you shortly.'

The elderly butler ushered them into an enormous room hung from floor to ceiling with large portraits in elaborate gold frames.

'Please make yourselves comfortable while I prepare refreshments.' He indicated the first portrait, a wizened old mouse with great pendulous whiskers. 'It is customary to begin here.'

Hermux and Birch gazed up obediently at the portrait. A brass plaque below it identified the subject as Roto Stepfitchler, Founder of the Stepfitchler Dynasty and Inventor of the Wheel.

'So that's old Roto,' said Hermux. 'He looks just like the history books. Quite the old guy. But the eyes are a little shifty.'

A wild clatter of pots and pans broke the heavy silence of the house. In the distance doors and drawers slammed open and shut. Silverware and dishes clashed. Glasses crashed. Then silence again.

Birch and Hermux looked at each other and shrugged. Then they moved on to the next portrait.

It was Rookum Stepfitchler, Inventor of the Compass.

'Dapper little guy,' said Hermux admiringly.

103

Then Hinkum Stepfitchler I, Inventor of the Printing Press.

Then Sir Boosik Stepfitchler, Discoverer of Gravity.

Kernel Stepfitchler, Founder of the University.

And Hinkum Stepfitchler II, Inventor of the Clock, the Microscope, the Telescope and the Gyroscope.

'This is like a fifth-grade history class,' said Hermux. 'Look, here's Boomboom Stepfitchler, the Inventor of the Steamboat. And Zizzo Stepfitchler, Discoverer of Electricity and Inventor of the Telephone. Cornum Stepfitchler, Inventor of the Tractor. And Miss Hissy Stepfitchler, Inventor of Dynamite. She looks like a tough old mouse.'

They stopped at Professor Stervin Stepfitchler, Translator of *The Book of Peas*.

'So this is him,' said Hermux. 'The great professor.' Professor Stepfitchler was an imposing figure seated behind an enormous desk piled high with enormous books. Birch was silent. He looked up at the painting nervously, as though he expected it to come to life and denounce him.

It looked to Hermux that it might indeed do just that. The eyes of the portrait glittered and glared down at them indignantly. The whole place was starting to give Hermux the heebie-jeebies.

'Refreshments are served,' the butler announced gloomily.

'Thank goodness,' Hermux told Birch under his breath. 'There are still three more walls to go. Is there anything they didn't invent?'

Chapter 34
LIKE FATHER, LIKE SON

Hinkum Stepfitchler's brightly lit desk occupied one end of the large vaulted library.

'Have a seat, gentlemen,' he said, without looking up. 'I'll be with you in a moment. I just want to finish this.'

Using a pair of tweezers, he picked up a tiny fragment of paper and held it up to the light. He examined it with a magnifying glass, turning it this way and that way.

'Aha!' he announced triumphantly. 'I knew I'd find it.' He placed the piece carefully in what looked like a jigsaw puzzle assembled on a sheet of glass. Then, very cautiously, he lowered another sheet of glass in place, fastened the two sheets together with large metal clips and turned it for Hermux and Birch to see.

'Finished!' he said with obvious pride.

Hermux leaned forward for a better look. It was a small water-stained piece of paper covered with rows of faded dots and scratches.

'Beautiful!' said Birch. 'Early Middle Mouse, I'd guess. Some sort of harvest prayer?'

'Very impressive,' said Hinkum. 'Ortolina tells me you've

got some sort of old manuscript you want to show me. Something terribly shocking. Although I'm afraid Pinchester may have had all the shock it can take for now. And may I ask how you got interested in old manuscripts?'

'I was a student of your father's.'

'Oh, yes, dear Father. And your name again?'

'Tentintrotter. Birch Tentintrotter.'

'*The* Tentintrotter?'

'I'm afraid so.'

Stepfitchler raised his magnifying glass and stared through it at Birch. His enormous eye looked thoroughly startled.

'I was under the impression that you were dead,' he said, finally.

'Well, as you can see, I'm not.'

'Apparently not.'

'I have to admit that I don't feel entirely comfortable coming to see you.'

'Now don't be ridiculous!' said Stepfitchler, putting down the magnifying glass. 'All that was years and years ago. Father was, as you remember, a bit rigid in his thinking. Particularly on certain subjects. But times have changed. And we have changed with them. We're considerably more open-minded today. Now I must say I am curious about what you've found this time. Surely it's not another Cat manuscript?'

'I'm afraid it is,' Birch admitted.

'Well, confound it! Let's see it!'

While Hinkum adjusted the light and Birch opened the scroll and unrolled it, Hermux studied the large map that covered the wall behind Hinkum's desk. Hermux found Pinchester. Then he followed the course of the Twisty River that ran inland north-west from Pinchester. He saw the straight line of the

106

Scarie Canal that ran due west from the Twisty and connected with the Shady River. He followed the curving line of the Longish River from its origins in the Lop-eared Mountains. Below the Shady there were a few towns and small cities. But the Great Desert and the upper stretches of the Longish River were completely uninhabited. The entire area was blank on the map. Hermux was surprised that it was shown at all. Most maps simply stopped at the Shady River. Folks weren't really interested in what was beyond that. It wasn't friendly country. Nothing but sand. People seldom went there. And those that did seldom returned.

'But somewhere in all that sand,' Hermux thought, 'may be the missing piece to this puzzle.'

'So you're saying that this supposed mouse revolution was so extreme that they managed to destroy every trace of evidence that the civilization of cats ever existed?' Hinkum sounded very interested in Birch's theory.

'Every trace of physical evidence,' explained Birch. 'The linguistic evidence still lingers. The word *cat* itself is evidence. It once referred to something.'

'I've always assumed it referred to a fantasy,' said Hinkum. 'A bad fantasy at that.'

'I believe it is more. And I think this scroll is the beginning of a trail that can lead us to the answer. That's why we're asking for your help. I want the university to allow us to compare the scroll with the map.'

'Oh, yes! The map!' said Hinkum eagerly. 'That's what started all this, isn't it?'

'It is.'

'And you've never given up, have you?'

Birch looked at Hermux. Hermux nodded encouragingly.

'No,' he said. 'I haven't. And I won't.'

'And you're asking the museum to underwrite a full-scale expedition to search for this lost library?'

'Right. With good planning and the original map, I think we can find it.'

'I'd like to examine the scroll more carefully in my laboratory. May I keep it for a short time?'

Birch hesitated.

'You've nothing to worry about. It won't leave the premises. And my home is quite secure, as you can see. Now, if you would, show me on my map where you've searched. And where you're planning to search again.'

Chapter 35
SURFACE TREATMENT

'We have an appointment with Mr Hutt,' Hermux explained to the bored receptionist. 'He's expecting us.'

Scaffolo Hutt's Salon de Fur occupied an entire brownstone building on Villum Avenue. His wealthy clientele included the most luxurious pelts in Pinchester.

'Believe me, Birch, first impressions really count with these people. Scaffolo will have you looking your best for the board meeting tonight.'

Moments later, Scaffolo appeared in his customary immaculately white jacket.

'Well, Hermux?' he asked with a polite smile. 'Who did you want me to see?'

Hermux pointed to Birch. Scaffolo froze in his tracks. His smile faded and was slowly replaced by a look of fascinated horror.

'I've never seen anything like this,' he said in a shaky voice. 'Was it some sort of awful chemical accident?'

Then he steeled himself and reached for the intercom. 'Code blue! Front desk! Stat!' And staff came running from every direction.

'Now I want everyone to remain absolutely calm,' Scaffolo commanded. 'Listen carefully! We can do this! But every moment counts. First of all, let's get him inside!'

Birch started to run for the front door, but a burly gopher collared him and set him firmly into a wheelchair and strapped him in place.

'Careful!' Scaffolo instructed. 'That fur looks as brittle as a chow mein noodle.'

Then Scaffolo began barking orders for lab tests, shampoos, hot oil treatments and conditioners. Plus a cut, colour, blow-dry and comb. As they wheeled Birch away, Scaffolo took Hermux aside and spoke to him in hushed tones.

'There's nothing you can do here. It may be hours before we know anything for sure. Why don't you go home and we'll call you?'

'I think I'll go shopping instead,' said Hermux.

'Splendid,' Scaffolo told him. 'Don't worry about your friend. He's pretty far gone, but we'll do everything we can!'

Hermux crossed Villum Avenue and headed straight for Orsik & Arrbale. He was considering a new look for Birch, and he knew just the right chipmunk to ask for help.

Tickin Rifflender had very definite ideas about fashion. Hermux had met her that past spring when she had helped him buy clothes for his undercover visit to the Last Resort. A fashion makeover for Birch was exactly the sort of challenge that Tickin enjoyed.

'Oh, I know the type!' she told Hermux when he explained the situation. 'He sounds just like my uncle Bopus. Excellent! Let's start with the shoes and build up from there.'

And she did.

Tickin chose black and white checked bucks with extremely pointy toes. And red socks.

'Yes!' she gloated.

Then the trousers.

'An outdoorsy type, right? We'll go with wool flannel. Big plaid. Big pleats. I'm seeing red and green.'

And she did.

'These will do nicely.' She grabbed a set of transparent plastic suspenders from a shelf.

'Now the shirt.' She paused for a moment with her eyes closed. 'I know just the thing.'

She vanished into the stockroom and returned with a toy-truck-yellow corduroy shirt.

'Micro-wale,' she explained. 'We'll top it with a burlap vest. Let's look at jackets.'

Hermux and Tickin agreed on a boxy, unconstructed sports coat in a burnt-orange oak-leaf suede. It had extra padding in the shoulders.

She laid out the entire outfit on the counter.

'So?' she asked. 'Bold, confident professor seeks financial support from arty aristocrats. What do you think?'

Chapter 36
EXPERT OPINION

'Dr Stepfitchler will now present his report,' Durrance Pootinall announced to the crowded boardroom. Flurty Palin whispered something naughty to Elusa Loitavender. She burst into a fit of giggles but stopped abruptly when she saw the dirty looks directed at her by both Tucka Mertslin and Skimpy Dormay. All eyes turned towards Hinkum.

'I have given the matter of Mr Tentintrotter and his mysterious manuscript very careful consideration,' he began, gesturing towards the end of the conference table where Birch, Mirrin and Hermux sat looking hopeful.

'As you know, Mr Tentintrotter is asking the museum to underwrite an expedition to the Great Desert with the hope of discovering a mysterious library, which he purports to be the sole surviving evidence of a lost civilization of cats. He bases his claims entirely on his own translation of this scroll. I have examined the scroll and tested it for authenticity. And I regret to report that it is a fake.'

'Oh, no!' said Mirrin.

'It's a sophisticated fake,' Hinkum continued, 'but a fake

nonetheless. The papyrus is the cleverest part. I estimate it to be about one hundred years old. The ink appears to be less than a year old. And the writing is gibberish. Quite amateurish, actually. I'm sure you all share my disappointment. The concept of a cat civilization and the possible existence of an entire library of cat texts and documents are exhilarating to say the least. And with Miss Stentrill's exhibit in progress, it's a very timely idea. Perhaps a bit too timely. If I didn't know Miss Stentrill better, I would swear that this has the feel of a publicity stunt.'

Hinkum stopped and looked wearily at Birch. Then he shook his head sadly. 'I am afraid, ladies and gentlemen, that we have been subjected to a hoax. I can only hope that our friends here have been similarly duped. Of course, it is not the first time that Mr Tentintrotter has jumped to a spectacular conclusion based on very flimsy evidence. However, I would have thought that he might have learned something from his earlier mistake.'

Hermux jumped to his feet angrily. 'But what about the map in the Stepfitchler Collection? Let's examine it and see if the writing is the same!'

'I'm afraid that's not possible,' Hinkum said calmly. 'The map was destroyed years ago. And besides, it was also a fake.'

'But how can you be so sure it was a fake?' demanded Hermux.

'Because, Mr Tantamoq, I was the one who drew it.'

'Oh, Hinkum, you devil!' Tucka purred. 'You're so bad!'

'That's outrageous!' Birch grumbled.

'I agree. And shameful. But it's the truth. I drew the map and left it in the library as a boyish prank. Unfortunately, when you found it, you took it much more seriously than I intended. Father tried to persuade you to drop the subject. And when you didn't,

113

I'm afraid he did what he had to do to protect the family name from scandal.'

'But he destroyed my career!'

'My sincere apologies,' said Hinkum. 'And now my suggestion to you is to let bygones be bygones and to burn this scroll immediately. It's completely worthless.'

Chapter 37
VERY DAIRY

'I know you're disappointed, Birch,' said Mirrin. 'We're all disappointed. But it's not the end of the world. We'll have a good dinner and figure out our next move. There it is, just ahead on the right.'

Mirrin turned the wheel sharply and brought her sporty new car to a sudden stop at the canopied entrance to the Choo-Choo Cheeserie.

'And look, they've got ballet parking for the Grand Opening.'

Sure enough, Teasila Tentriff herself came bounding down the walk in a long white tutu. Holding both arms high over her head, she circled the car in a series of lightning-fast twirls and finished with a flying leap over the bonnet to the driver's side. Then, balancing on one foot as she extended her tail straight up into the air, she bent forward at the waist and reached out gracefully to open Mirrin's door.

'Why, thank you, Teasila,' Mirrin told her, handing her the keys. 'That was wonderful. Now, be careful parking this thing. It's brand new, and it's very spunky.'

She looked proudly at both Birch and Hermux as Teasila

roared off into the parking lot. Hermux was as neat as a pin, of course. And Birch? Well, the afternoon at Scaffolo Hutt's had completely transformed him. His drab and dry fur glowed with new silky suppleness. The bold white stripes above his rusty cheeks made his eyes look especially dark and romantic. And with the fur on his forehead fluffed out and spiked up, his missing ear only added to a sporty and slightly rakish air. But despite it all, he looked miserable.

'Now, you two, listen to me,' Mirrin said sternly. 'I believe in you, Birch. I believe the scroll is genuine. And so does Hermux. I don't know what Hinkum is up to, but it's time to move to Plan B. So we've got to figure out what Plan B is. And we're not going to figure out anything moping around like a bunch of failures. Right now we're going to march in there and have a good time and eat ourselves a good cheese dinner. Then we're going to come up with a new idea.'

Luckily Mirrin had made reservations early in the week, because the Choo-Choo Cheeserie was absolutely packed. For Hermux it was love at first sight. There were tiny trains everywhere. Locomotives chugged along the edge of the bar. They rumbled across trestle bridges that ran from table to table. They circled booths, rattling the salt and pepper shakers and tomato-sauce bottles and napkin holders. They stopped at stations and crossings and rolled past scale model farms with lit houses and open barns. They crossed plains and mountains and roared through sleepy towns and villages. Their engines puffed. Their whistles blew. And each and every flatcar carried a delicious cargo of cheese.

Yellow cheese. And white cheese. Crumbly cheese. And creamy cheese. Sweet cheese. And stinky cheese. By the time

116

they were seated in their booth, Hermux had completely forgotten Birch's scroll and all about the kingdom of the cats.

'This is a great booth,' he said gleefully. 'Look how tightly the tracks curve here. They'll have to slow the trains down to get around it.'

As though to prove his point, a heavily laden train lumbered into view at that moment and began to work its way around their table at a leisurely pace. Hermux took a slice of very sharp Cheddar. And a piece of aged Parmesan. And a bit of blue cheese. He nibbled happily on each of them and looked around at the crowd. He was surprised to see that almost everyone was looking back at him. Or rather they were looking at Mirrin. Her show had made her a celebrity in Pinchester. A steady stream of people began to drop by the table to say hello and offer congratulations on the success of her show. There was definitely a party in the air at the Choo-Choo Cheeserie. After a while even Birch seemed to relax and lighten up in the boisterous atmosphere.

Then the restaurant door opened, and a wave of whispers swept through the restaurant.

'Uh-oh!' Hermux warned Mirrin and Birch. 'There's Tucka. And she's with Rink Firsheen.'

Chapter 38
LARGER THAN LIFE

Tucka was surprisingly oblivious to the stares she drew in her transparent pink vinyl raincoat.

Birch turned to look, but Mirrin shifted in her seat and blocked his view. 'I can only hope that that's a body stocking she's wearing under that,' she said, plucking a pawful of grapes from the fruit caboose and offering them to Birch.

'It's hard to tell from here,' said Hermux with a squint. 'Something's up, though. I've never seen Tucka miss the chance of enjoying a scene she was making. I'll bet they're planning something. I hope it's not our lobby again.'

Rink Firsheen was Pinchester's most sought-after designer. The handsome otter was Tucka's personal architect and creative adviser. He carried a large roll of drawings that he opened and spread across their table, while Tucka grabbed unsuccessfully for a wedge of Brie from a passing train.

'I wish I could get close enough to see what they're doing,' said Hermux. 'Can I get you something from the bar?'

'I'll have a Frosted Turnip with lots of salt,' said Mirrin. 'Birch?'

'A Bitter Acorn on ice, please.' As Hermux manoeuvred his

way through the crowd, Birch took Mirrin's paw in his. 'Thank you for sticking with me,' he told her solemnly. 'I feel like I've landed you in the frying pan again.'

'I like a good fight, Birch, if I believe in what I'm fighting for. And I believe in you. I always have.'

Hermux took advantage of the noisy throng at the bar to work his way close to Rink and Tucka's booth. He positioned himself behind a large potted milkweed and focused his ears on their conversation.

Tucka was riled up.

'What a bunch of pretentious bores,' she told Rink. 'I'll show them what a museum can be! I'm sick to death of small people and small ideas. I hate "tiny"! I despise "petite"! I want "larger than life"!'

She caught sight of a trainload of walnut cheese balls heading their way. But scowled as it switched tracks at the last minute and disappeared into a tunnel.

'From now on I want monumental! And if I have to build my own museum, I'll do it!' She snapped her fingers gleefully. 'That's it, Rink! I'll build my own. The Tucka Mertslin Museum of Monumental Art! We'll only show the biggest art in the world!'

'Of course!' Rink exclaimed. 'Colossal art! No more mini art!' He grabbed a napkin and began sketching in broad, sure strokes. 'You enter through a huge hall and then there is a long marble pool framed by rows and rows of tremendous columns, and reflected in the pool, lit very mysteriously, of course, is a really humongous statue. The biggest one we can find.'

'I think I have a lead on just the right statue,' she said coyly.

'Good!' said Rink.

Hermux's ears twitched, and he pressed closer.

'It's a gigantic statue!' Tucka boasted.

'Wonderful!' crowed Rink.

'It's never been seen in public!'

'Marvellous!'

'It's totally shocking!'

'Perfect!'

Hermux's nose itched.

'It may be twenty-four carat gold!'

'Outstanding!'

'It's the lost mummy of the king of the cats!' Tucka purred, and watched Rink's face for his reaction.

Rink choked on a mouthful of mozzarella.

'That should take the wind out of Mirrin Stentrill's sails,' Tucka gloated as Rink reached frantically for his water.

'How do you do it?' he sputtered in admiration.

'Ruthless devotion to my public,' she said modestly. 'Now, Rink, this is absolutely confidential. The statue is going to be a special gift from a very special new friend. I'm leaving tomorrow to pick it up, and I don't want you saying a word about it to anyone.'

A trainload of fragrant pecorino was just beginning to pick up speed in front of Tucka. She inserted her fork between two cars and deftly flicked her wrist. There was a screech of metal on metal as the train left the tracks in a shower of sparks and derailed on the table.

'Looks like we've had an accident,' she announced innocently. She popped a piece of cheese into her mouth and smiled. 'Now let's see the plans for the Wild Girl promotion. The timing couldn't be better.'

Someone jostled Hermux from behind.

'Hey, what are you doing there?' demanded a gruff voice.

120

Hermux struggled to disentangle himself from the potted milkweed.

'I was on my way to the bar, and I dropped a piece of Cheshire,' Hermux explained lamely. He turned and found himself face to face with a grim little middle-aged mouse in a conductor's uniform. The mouse tapped his foot impatiently. He looked familiar to Hermux. But he couldn't quite place him.

'Cheshire is my favourite cheese,' Hermux told him sheepishly. 'Well, I should get our drinks and get back to my table. People will wonder what's happened to me.'

The conductor watched Hermux dubiously as he pushed his way towards the bar.

'Now, where have I seen that mouse?' Hermux asked himself. 'I think it had something to do with the museum.'

Chapter 39
THE WEE HOURS

'It was horrible,' Hermux told Terfle. 'We were finished eating, so we weren't paying any attention to the trains. I didn't even notice the doll until the train stopped right in front of us, and suddenly there she is on the last car. A little grey mouse doll dressed in a beret and an artist's smock. Sprawled across a stack of sliced provolone. She's holding a painter's palette with tiny dabs of paint. "Look how cute! Mirrin, somebody sent you a doll!" I say, and then I see the doll's other hand. It's holding a paintbrush. And somebody has driven the paintbrush through the doll's heart. And then poured on tomato sauce.

'So Mirrin lets out a shriek. And that's when I remembered where I had seen that stubby mouse in the conductor's uniform. He's the one that started the riot at the art museum. The one from the Brotherhood of Mice. A mouse supremacist or whatever. Birch and I scoured the place looking for him. But there was no sign of him. Of course, I have to suspect Tucka too. It certainly had her touch. But why would she do it? What do you think?'

Terfle sat silent. Then she walked over to her empty food bowl and nudged it impatiently with her antennae.

'All right,' Hermux said. 'I know you can't think on an empty stomach. I just wanted to bring you up to date.'

He opened a new tin of dried aphids and scooped a hefty serving into Terfle's bowl.

'Anyway, we can talk in the morning. It was quite an evening, and I'm beat. I'm turning in.'

Hermux got into bed. He made a short entry in his journal.

Thank you for old friends. For ballerinas and beauty shops and department stores. For restaurants and railroads. Thank you for fizzy drinks and for the remarkable variety of cheeses that are available.

Then he switched off the lamp. But he didn't go to sleep right away. He lay there looking at the ceiling. The night was very dark. A new moon. Even when his eyes adjusted, the blackness was impenetrable. But it wasn't quite empty. And it wasn't quite still. There seemed to be something there that wanted to be seen.

Hermux got up and turned on his tulip blossom night light. The warm glow made his room seem safe and familiar again. Then he got back into bed, closed his eyes, and fell asleep.

★ ★ ★

Mirrin tossed and turned, but sleep would not come. Finally she got up. She made a cup of tea and turned on the lights in her studio. The doll had been a nasty shock. Crude and invasive. And public. It angered her.

She stood at her drawing table for a long time without moving. She closed her eyes and concentrated on the darkness.

123

Somewhere in the distance a train wailed. Mirrin opened her eyes and chose a thick, black crayon.

She began to draw. A reclining figure slowly emerged from the white ground. The torso turned slightly. An arm thrown out to the side. The legs extended, crossed at the ankle. The blank face tilted up. The outline of a garment. The drape and the shadow. The lines of a hat. One hand holding something roundish and flat. The other clutched to the chest. The features of the face. More and more familiar. Then colour. Cool highlights in the silver fur. A ring of primaries on the palette. A crimson stain on the smock.

'You can shock us,' she said. 'You can scare us. But we will not run.'

★ ★ ★

The Scarvent Hotel wasn't very big. It wasn't especially nice either. But it was quiet. And it was clean. Mostly.

'You got a call while you were out, Mr Tentintrotter,' the night clerk said. 'A gentleman. He didn't leave a message.'

'Did he say he'd call back?'

'Nope. Just hung up.'

'What time?'

'About an hour ago.'

'That's strange.'

'Expecting someone?'

'Not really.'

In the elevator Birch hummed an old show tune. Mirrin used to sing it in college. He was feeling pretty good. Surprising, considering that in the last four hours he'd been called a liar and

124

a swindler in public and Mirrin had been served a gruesome threat for dessert.

'Still,' he thought, unlocking the door to his room, 'I'm not giving up. And Mirrin's not giving up on me. That's what counts.'

He was smiling as he stepped inside. He didn't hear the footsteps behind him in the hallway. He didn't see the blow coming. He didn't even feel it.

Chapter 40
ROTTEN LUCK

He dreamed of clover. As far as he could see. Fields of woolly green leaves. Itchy, woolly green leaves spinning him around and around. It made him woozy.

Birch opened his eyes and sneezed. It was daylight, and his head ached something awful. He was lying face down on the clover carpet. He tried to roll over, and everything went blurry. He closed his eyes again.

'Oh!' he said miserably. He felt the lump on his head. 'Ouch!'

He tried to remember what he was doing on the floor. He remembered coming back to the hotel. He remembered opening the door. He remembered something about clover.

He braced his paws and slowly, slowly worked his way to sitting up.

He took a deep breath and opened his eyes.

The room was a mess.

His clothes were everywhere. The mattress was thrown on the floor. The bureau was overturned. Birch struggled to his feet and staggered to his desk, afraid of what he would find.

The drawers stood open. And empty.

'The scroll!' he groaned. 'My notebooks!' He sat down heavily in the chair. He thought about what Mirrin would say. About Hermux. About disappointing them. About disappointing himself. Birch thought about failing at everything he tried. His eyes brimmed with tears. Maybe he should run away.

'No,' he told himself. 'Not this time.'

He made himself get up. He went to the bathroom and washed his face. He held a cold washcloth to the back of his head. Then he switched on the light and looked at himself in the mirror. His eyes were bloodshot. His whiskers were bent like rusty wire.

There was a note pinned to his jacket.

Listen up, chipmunk!
Stay out of mouse business!
And stay out of Pinchester!

the Brotherhood of Mice

He called Mirrin.

As soon as Birch hung up, Mirrin called Hermux and drove straight to the hotel. Hermux left his pancakes sitting on the table and ran all the way. Mirrin arrived first. She ordered Birch right into bed. She ordered the manager to send up more pillows. She ordered the bellhop to get a bucket of ice. She ordered Hermux to go and get coffee and aspirin.

Mirrin refused to listen to Birch's apology.

'You don't have to apologize to me for getting hit over the

127

head by a bunch of fanatics. Why would any of us think that someone would want to steal a scroll that no one's ever heard of? A scroll that's officially a fake? No, Birch Tentintrotter, something strange is going on here.'

She plumped his pillows and handed him the ice pack.

'Now, just hold this where it hurts,' she told him. 'You're right about the police. I don't think we're very high on Mayor Pinkwiggin's priority list. If he got the scroll back, he'd probably burn it.'

Hermux came back with coffee and the morning paper.

'You're not going to believe this,' he said, holding up the front page.

GO WEST, WILD GIRL!
Tucka Mertslin Begins Promotional Tour of Western River Towns

A Moozella Corkin Exclusive

She's the face that launched a thousand products. Now she's launching herself. Tomorrow morning, Tucka Mertslin – that's Captain Mertslin to you, mate! – takes the helm of the SS *Beauty Queen* and steams out of Pinchester with a full cargo of big-city glamour and Wild Girl cosmetics for the wild folks out west.

'It's an all-singing, all-dancing,

all-Western spectacular, featuring me, of course,' said Tucka, relaxing on her new showboat after an exhausting rehearsal. Captain Mertslin looked positively dangerous in her new Wild Girl Sandy Lip Gloss and Prickly Pear Fur Bristle. 'I wear fabulous costumes, sing fabulous songs, and do a little sharpshooting, fancy roping and knife throwing.'

The show also features a twelve-piece banjo orchestra and the Wild Girl Dancers.

'There's a Wild Girl in every woman,' says Mertslin. 'And I'm aiming to set her free. I know it's a big undertaking. But we've refitted the *Beauty Queen* with three state-of-the-art beauty salons. We'll be doing makeovers wherever we go. This is my missionary work. There's so much ugliness in this world. And I'm just trying to do my part to help.'

So bon voyage, Tucka! And y'all come back real soon, y'hear?

Tucka Mertslin's Wild Girl Beauty Products are available at Orsik & Arrbale.

'How does she do it?' asked Hermux. 'And what are we going to do? She's making a beeline for the Longish River, and she'll be there in a week.'

'Is she really a problem?' asked Birch.

Hermux and Mirrin looked at each other.

'Yes!' they said.

'Tucka is a big problem,' Mirrin went on. 'She's smart. She's determined. And now she's got plans for a very big statue.'

'Stepfitchler must have told her about it,' Hermux said. 'I just know it. He's promised her the king's mummy for her museum. But how does he know where it is?'

'He probably has the original map. The one he claims he forged.'

An awful picture formed itself in Hermux's mind. It was a painting of Hinkum Stepfitchler III standing in front of a desert tent. Beneath it was a plaque that read, 'Inventor of Modern Archeology. Founder of the Stepfitchler Museum of Lost Civilizations'.

'I think I know what's going on,' Hermux said. He explained.

'Why would he do that?' asked Mirrin.

'Because he doesn't have his portrait yet,' said Birch. 'He's the world's foremost authority on Old Mouse. But he needs something bigger than that to measure up to the Stepfitchler Dynasty.'

'But then who robbed you?' asked Mirrin. 'Hinkum could have just copied the scroll while he had it. And we would never have known. Besides, does he even need the scroll? He's already got the map. Birch, do you need some more ice?'

Birch shook his head. His headache was slowly going away. He watched Hermux pacing the floor.

130

'What we really need is the map,' Birch said. 'And a way to get there ahead of Tucka.'

'There's not much we can do about the map,' said Hermux. 'But if we can figure out where they're going, I think I've got a way to get there ahead of them. I'm going to call Linka Per-flinger. She owes me a favour.'

Chapter 41
AIRBORNE

'You're sure you're comfortable back there, Birch?'

'Just fine.'

'Everyone buckled in?'

Hermux checked his seat belt for the third time.

'All right! We're off!'

Linka eased back the throttle, and the plane began to move away from the hangar. Hermux kept one eye on Linka and the other on the runway. It was difficult to tell which was more exciting: sitting so close to Linka that their whiskers touched, or taking his first ride in an aeroplane.

As nervous as he was about both situations, Hermux found himself humming right along with the engine as the bright silver plane taxied for takeoff. It was the perfect tune for the beginning of a beautiful day.

His stomach gave a swoop as the plane left the ground and accelerated into its climb. It whirled to the left as the plane banked to the right. It dropped down to the floor as the plane lurched in a sudden updraught. Hermux stopped humming and closed his eyes. Maybe it wasn't going to be such a beautiful day after all.

He felt a tap on his knee.

'It'll smooth out in a minute,' Linka shouted above the engine. 'Once we make our altitude. In the meantime, don't close your eyes. Keep them on the horizon. And don't forget to breathe.'

Hermux looked straight ahead, past the blur of the propeller, out into open space. He took a deep breath, and he began to feel better. Ahead of them, the Twisty River ran true to its name, zigzagging north-west from Pinchester to the Scarie Canal. Once Tucka crossed the canal, it would be smooth sailing and downstream from then on. Tucka had a four-day head start, but Linka was confident they would get ahead of her.

'Leave it to me,' she said. And she'd meant it. When Hermux asked Linka for help, she had only hesitated for a moment. 'You know that this kind of adventure demands careful planning,' she told him seriously. 'It's my favourite kind. And I'm very good at it. All right. Count me in.'

She sat down that minute and began to make lists. She made a list of food and medicine; a list of maps they would need; a list of what Hermux should pack (including a sun hat, cotton socks, and three pairs of underwear); a list of spare parts for the plane; a list of things to do; a list of things to get; a list of questions that needed answers; a list of things that could go wrong. And finally, a list of all the lists.

The afternoon before departure, they all met at Mirrin's and went over each list, one item at a time, until every item on every list was crossed through and checked off. Except for one small item at the bottom of Linka's personal list.

The item read: Note to T –

The next morning after breakfast she finally sat down at her desk and wrote it.

Dear Turfip,

*Welcome back, dear. I hope the
conference went well. I've got to be gone for
a few days. Nothing serious. Just catching
up with some old friends.*

Fondly,

Linka

Then she stopped by his apartment on her way to the airport and left it in his mailbox.

'It's true for the most part,' she thought. She checked her altimeter and levelled the plane out. 'They are old friends. At least they seem like old friends now. I just hope he takes it well.' She cut back the throttle and the engine dropped down into a steady, familiar drone. She was right on course above the river. One at a time she stretched her paws away from the stick. It felt so much better to be at the controls of a plane instead of a typewriter. She loosened her seat belt a little and settled back comfortably. It was a wonderful day for flying.

She looked over at Hermux and smiled. He was staring out of the window. Hermux really did seem like a nice mouse. He was an excellent watchmaker. She glanced down at her watch. It hadn't lost a minute in six months. He certainly didn't talk as much as Turfip did. That was nice. He had a pleasant voice and very good manners. His friends were very interesting. Mirrin especially. And it promised to be an excellent adventure. A lost civilization. A forgotten library. And cats! It gave her goose-bumps to think about it. The whole idea of cats was exciting. They might be disgusting, but she wasn't the least bit afraid of them – dead or alive. Well, dead at least ...

She looked back to check on Birch. He was sound asleep, wedged between the tents and the sleeping bags.

Hermux turned back from the window. He gave her a little wave.

'It's very beautiful from up here,' he said, mouthing the words distinctly.

'Feeling better?' she asked.

He nodded and smiled.

He had a sweet little smile. He also smelled good. Something clean and outdoorsy. Like fresh-mown hay.

Chapter 42
FLIGHT PATH

It was late at night. Hermux had gone to the library to return a book that was overdue. He owed a fine of sixty-three dollars. He counted it out carefully. But there was no one at the desk to take his money. In fact, there didn't seem to be anyone anywhere. The library was completely empty. 'It's awfully dark and quiet in here,' he thought. 'Maybe it's closed.' Then he saw a lamp burning on a table at the far end of the reading room. Someone was sitting at the table. Hermux went closer and, as he approached, he could make out a figure hunched over an old map unrolled across the table. 'Excuse me,' Hermux said. 'Do you work here?' Very slowly the figure turned towards him, revealing a broad face with long fur, tabby stripes and a pair of cold, calculating eyes. It smiled an evil, snarlish grin and unsheathed a paw full of gleaming claws. Hermux tried to run, but his feet seemed miles and miles away. 'Help!' he tried to shout. 'Help! Run! It's a cat!' Then a deafening growl filled the air, and he felt an awful thump.

Hermux woke with a start. What a relief! It was late afternoon. They were still high in the air.

'Sorry about that!' Linka said. 'We hit an air pocket. Did you get any sleep?'

Hermux nodded. 'More than I wanted,' he said. 'Where are we?'

Linka pointed down. Below them a clean, straight line of water pointed west like a silver arrow. 'We're coming to the end of the canal. Then we'll head south-east along the Shady. There's an airport at Boomerville. We'll put down there for the night. It's about another hour.'

'Are you OK? Aren't you tired?'

'Too happy to be tired. It feels so good to be flying again.' She patted the console. 'This is my baby. And I've missed her.'

Linka nodded towards the thermos beside her.

'There's coffee if you want some.'

'Thanks,' Hermux said.

'I haven't heard a peep out of Birch. That's good. I was afraid he'd be the nervous type.'

Hermux leaned over and poured himself some coffee. His whiskers brushed against Linka's face. 'Excuse me,' he said. Hermux sipped his coffee and looked out of the window. He had a big smile on his face. It was a beautiful world. They were flying over farmland. The Scarie Canal ran right through the heart of pea country. The land on both sides of the canal was neatly parcelled into squares as far as the horizon. The squares were ploughed into lines. Some of the lines ran north and south. Some east and west. And some were diagonal. Hermux thought it looked like someone had thrown a brown and grey quilt down on each side of the canal for a big picnic.

'Have you ever flown over this in the spring?' he asked.

'Oh, yes!' Linka said. 'Wonderful. Every shade of green.

Little peas, split peas, chickpeas, black-eyed peas, snow peas. And sweet peas, of course. My favourite. Once I flew across on a warm evening in early summer. The smell of sweet peas filled the sky.'

Hermux was very fond of sweet peas himself. 'Have you had many adventures out this way?' he asked.

'A few. Well, four actually, if you count flying Mrs Lonick out for her son's wedding.'

'Bierthinna Lonick?'

'That's her!'

'You were alone with her all day in this little plane?'

'That's right. She didn't want to fly with me, but she had no choice. And she never let me forget it for one moment that we were in the air.'

'Once a year I have to go out to her house and clean all eleven of her clocks,' said Hermux. 'She watches me every minute I'm there. And she never fails to remind me that I'm just not the watchmaker that my father was. Which doesn't surprise her a bit "because children today are single-mindedly deter-mined to be a bitter disappointment to their parents".'

Linka laughed. '"I don't approve of women flying,"' she snorted, imitating Mrs Lonick. '"The only reason I'm in this ridiculous machine, and don't you forget it, Missy, is because my imbecile son doesn't have the common courtesy to marry someone closer to home. And I'm not about to spend a week on a train for what is undoubtedly going to be a dull wedding with an even duller bride. Now you just wipe that smug smile off your face and get us there without smashing us to smith-ereens."'

Hermux said, 'I guess you get all sorts of adventures.'

'Well, I didn't know whether to laugh or cry with Mrs Lonick. I guess I did both.'

'Do you ever get scared? Flying those supplies to Dr Dandiffer's expedition in the jungle sounded pretty dangerous.'

Linka turned and looked at Hermux very seriously. There was something so likeable about her face. Her eyes were a nutty, chocolate brown. Almost the same colour as her fur. And her nose was so cute. A tiny bit crooked. Hermux wanted to lean over and rub it with his.

'I don't usually tell anyone this,' she said. 'I certainly can't ever tell Turfip. But I think you'll understand, Hermux. I do get scared. Often. But I can't let it stop me. Or I might as well give up. I try to only take reasonable risks. But sometimes to get my job done I don't have a choice. I just have to do it.'

Hermux was surprised. He thought it over. So even adventurers get scared. But they have to go on.

Far below them, the farmland was giving way to the rolling green hills that flanked the broad valley of the Shady River.

The sun was setting. On the road that ran alongside the river, Hermux began to see the tiny lights of tiny cars. It looked so peaceful. Looking down from here, it was hard to believe that there was danger anywhere in the world.

'You're very brave,' he said. 'I admire that. I admire you.' He stopped himself before he got carried away.

Behind them Birch coughed and snorted. Then he went back to his steady snore.

Linka smiled. Then she pointed excitedly out her window.

'Look!' she said. 'We're in luck! There they are! And we're right behind them.'

'Where?' said Hermux.

'There! See the smoke?' Linka banked the plane, and Hermux could see a white plume of smoke drifting along the north bank of the river. At the head of it, smokestacks puffing, steamed the SS *Beauty Queen*.

An enormous painted banner hung over its side.

BOOMERVILLE
BIG SHOW
TONIGHT!

Chapter 43
LINE-UP

From his perch on the top deck of the SS *Beauty Queen*, a wiry gopher in a mustard-yellow suit barked at the rowdy crowd below.

'Step right up and get your tickets, folks! The show starts in fifteen short minutes! Direct from Pinchester – the beauty capital of the world! Tucka Mertslin and her Wild Girl Revue! One night only! Featuring the Prairie Moon Banjo Orchestra under the direction of Swade Sletchin. It's a rootin', tootin', sharp-shootin' extravaganza! You'll never forget it as long as you live! Don't put it off a moment longer! It's a sellout crowd! Get your tickets now! All singing! All dancing! All beeeeeeautiful wild girls!'

Hermux, Linka and Birch stared up at the blazing lights of the showboat. It looked much bigger from ground level than it had from the air. It was easily five storeys tall, and it was lit up like a birthday cake. Somehow Hermux had pictured it much smaller and much darker and much easier to sneak around.

'I think it would look better if you got the tickets,' Linka told him, giving him a slight nudge in the direction of the ticket booth.

'Oh!' said Hermux. 'Of course! I'll get the tickets.'

A showboat was always a festive occasion in Boomerville. But the arrival of Tucka's Wild Girl Revue couldn't have been better timed. The farmers were in town, and they were ready to celebrate. The peas were harvested. The crop had been good. And after a summer of hard work out in the sun, there wasn't a farm wife in the county that wasn't ready for a new fur style, a tube of paw softener, some bubble bath and a bottle of perfume.

Hermux looked around at the fresh-scrubbed faces and found the people of Boomerville immensely likeable. He got in line behind a family of river rats. A mother, father and two little girls. The older girl held a book tightly clasped under her arm. She was shouting angrily at her little sister.

'She is too!'

'She is not!' her little sister shouted back.

'She is too!'

The little sister made frantic grab for the book, knocking it from her sister's grasp. It fell to the ground at Hermux's feet. He picked it up to return it and saw on its cover a photograph of Tucka Mertslin.

'What's this?' he asked.

'It's my Tucka scrapbook,' the little girl told him proudly. She dusted it off and inspected it for damage. She glared at her sister. 'Tucka Mertslin is the most beautiful woman in the world!'

'She is not!' her little sister screamed.

'She is too! I'm going to get her autograph!' she confided to Hermux.

'You are not!'

'I am too!'

142

'Girls!' the mother chided. 'Don't bother the nice man. Let's go now. And Thirspin, you leave your sister's scrapbook alone.'

As soon as the mother turned away, the older sister stuck out her tiny pink tongue in triumph. Then the younger sister raised her foot and furiously stomped the other's tail.

'Mummy!' she shrieked.

'Three adults, please!' Hermux told the ticket-hamster with relief.

The hamster chewed furiously on a pencil while he counted out the tickets and a dollar in change.

'I think you owe me another dollar,' said Hermux politely. 'That was an eight-dollar bill I gave you.'

The ticket-hamster removed the splintered pencil stub from his mouth. 'Nope,' he said, without a pause. 'It was a seven.' He smiled an unfriendly, uneven smile that revealed a mouthful of lead paste and pencil pulp. Then he leaned over and spat into a tin can. 'Enjoy the show!' he said. 'Next!'

Hermux could see that there was no point in arguing. He walked away with as much dignity as he could muster.

'Watch your wallets!' he warned Linka and Birch. 'This is a slippery bunch.'

They started up the gangway. Linka stopped and pointed downriver towards the last faint glow of the sunset. 'Look how beautiful that is,' she said loudly. Then she lowered her voice. 'Now, Birch, you talk to the crew and see if you can find out exactly where they're going and how soon they plan to get there. Hermux, you check out the staterooms. I'm going to try to get backstage and see what I can learn.'

The lights on the boat dimmed and came up again.

'They're getting ready to start the show,' said Hermux. 'Good luck, both of you, and be careful.'

Chapter 44
MIRROR IMAGE

Linka waited for the overture to begin. Then she opened the stage door and slipped inside. She found herself in a narrow hallway jammed full of boxes and crates and racks of costumes. The air was stale and musty. She slipped into the shadows behind a steamer trunk and looked around to get her bearings.

As the banjo orchestra swung into a nerve-splitting polka, Linka rehearsed her story one more time. 'I am a cub reporter for the *Boomerville Bugle*. This is my very first big story. I'm calling it "After the Applause – The Real Lives of Today's Glamorous Show People". Anything they can tell me about day-to-day life on the boat would be a big help. Like where they are going exactly. When do they plan to get there? What does Tucka do all day? Where is her cabin? Is it hard to get to? Is it unattended during the performance? Is anyone unusual travelling with her? Have they noticed anything peculiar at all on the trip so far?'

'All right,' she thought. 'I've got it down. Now let's get to work.'

She crept forward, wrinkling her nose and following the unmistakable trail of rose-scented face powder that drifted towards her. It led her to a door that was slightly ajar. The room inside was brightly lit. A sheet of paper was taped to the door.

NOTICE TO PERFORMERS

1. No chewing gum, twigs, sticks, or grasses anywhere backstage or onstage.

2. No whining about wages, schedules, rehearsals, workloads, or additional assigned duties.

3. Please respect Miss Mertslin's personal space at all times. No touching, speaking, or eye contact unless specifically requested.

4. Missed rehearsals will result in immediate termination.

5. <u>ALL FLOWERS, CANDY AND MISCELLANEOUS</u> <u>GIFTS OF ANY KIND ARE THE EXCLUSIVE</u> <u>PROPERTY OF TUCKA MERTSLIN COSMETICS</u>. Please turn them in promptly. (DON'T THINK WE'RE NOT WATCHING YOU!)

6. Visit the Tucka Mertslin outlet store on Deck 3 and take advantage of our generous employee discount (3%).

7. All off-brand cosmetics will be confiscated and destroyed.

8. Have a nice day!

  Be on time! Or pay the fine!

The Management

'These boots are killing me,' someone in the room complained. 'They're two sizes too small.'

145

Linka put her hand on the doorknob and pushed the door just the tiniest bit further open to see who was talking.

'If you're going to come in, then come in!' bawled a husky voice. 'Don't just stand there! You're already late!'

Linka stepped inside uncertainly. It was a small room crowded with mirrors and dressing tables and brilliantly lit by rows and rows of lightbulbs. Seated at the first table, a very plump mouse in a blue gingham dress eyed Linka angrily. She blotted her lips carefully on a tissue and got to her feet.

'Get in here! And get ready!' she told Linka impatiently. 'We're on right after Tucka's monologue. You've barely got time to get dressed.' She dabbed her face with an enormous powder puff.

Linka sneezed.

'Excuse me!' she said.

'It's too late for excuses! You were supposed to be here this afternoon. And look at you! You're ridiculous! You're much too thin! And much too young!'

There were two more mice dressed in the same costume. One of them was putting on what looked like layers and layers of false eyelashes. The other was struggling to pull on a high-heeled orange boot tooled with green flowers and cacti.

'You missed rehearsal,' the first mouse went on. 'So you'll have to fake it for tonight. Just stay out of Tucka's way when she starts her high kick. Or you'll end up like Pluff did last night. Two chipped teeth and a broken nose.'

A thrum of banjos onstage was met by thunderous applause.

'Get a move on! That's Tucka's entrance,' the mouse told her. 'Oh, by the way, I'm Chintsy. Chintsy Tureen. And this is Dureetha.' She pointed to the mouse in eyelashes. 'And that's

Shanell.' Then she stood back and looked at Linka suspiciously. 'Say, where did you dance before this?'

Linka thought for a moment. 'Well, I began my studies with Teasila Tentriff in Pinchester –'

'Oh, get me an aspirin!' Dureetha groaned. 'Just what we need, another princess of the snowflakes!'

'But I got kicked out,' Linka added quickly.

'Oh? And why was that?'

'I ... uhhh ... I wore my tutu too short.'

'You mean your tutu was too-too?'

'Much much too-too!' Linka said mischievously.

'This is sounding better. Then what?'

'Well, I moved around. Danced a little here. Danced a little there. Shows. Clubs. I just finished up a gig at the Wiggle Inn up in Twyrp.'

'So why'd you leave Twyrp?'

'I wasn't seeing nose to nose with the boss, if you know what I mean.'

'Honey, I know exactly what you mean,' said Chintsy. Dureetha and Shanell nodded sympathetically.

'That's one thing about this job you don't have to worry about. Tucka's as mean as a snake and as cheap as a gopher. No offence. But she leaves us alone. As long as we weigh in ten kilograms heavier and look five years older than her, she's happy. Which is going to be a big problem for you, kid. You'll have to put some weight on fast. And lose the fresh face.'

There was a loud knock on the door. 'Five minutes, ladies!' the stage manager growled. 'And look lively! Tucka's got a mood thing going!'

'That's your table and mirror. Get your make-up on, and we'll get you dressed.'

147

Linka sat down and looked at herself in the mirror. She opened her purse and ran a brush quickly over her face. Then she dabbed some clear gloss on her lips. She looked up to see Chintsy, Dureetha, and Shanell watching her in amazement.

'What?' she said.

'Your make-up.'

'I don't usually wear a lot,' Linka explained.

'You do now,' Chintsy told her. 'Dureetha, hand me that eyeliner. And you just hold still, Miss ... What is your name, anyway?'

'Edwitha,' Linka said. 'Edwitha Branspiller.'

Chintsy scowled. Dureetha rolled her eyes.

'But that's not my stage name, of course.' The three dancers looked at her expectantly. Linka thought hard. She narrowed her eyes. Then she smiled lazily. 'My stage name is Twitchi Tiptail,' she said. 'My friends call me Twitch.'

Chapter 45
WHERE NEVER IS HEARD
A DISCOURAGING WORD

The theatre was completely packed, and the crowd was excited. It looked to Hermux like all of Boomerville had turned out for the show. And Linka had been dead right about dressing for the occasion. The men all wore plaid shirts, freshly laundered overalls, little straw hats and bright neckerchiefs. Hermux breathed a sigh of relief. After their whirlwind shopping stop at Crawfig's General Store, he fitted right in. He loved his new peas-in-the-pod printed neckerchief and his straw hat with the shiny blue hatband.

He finally found a table near the back and took his seat just as the gaslight chandeliers began to flicker and fade.

The waiter was a woodchuck.

'Last call for drinks before the show!' he barked.

'Could I get a tall Beet Blossom with no ice?' Hermux whispered.

Banjos began a lonesome waltz and the red velvet curtain slowly opened to reveal a stark prairie scene. Overhead a huge night sky blazed with stars. Silhouetted against a line of fence stood the solitary figure of Tucka Mertslin, her face dramatically lit by what appeared to be a single moonbeam. She wore tight purple sequinned trousers and a bolero jacket with 'Wild Girl' embroidered across the front in bold letters. Her face was framed by a ghostly white ten-gallon hat ringed in a mirror-ball fringe. She twirled a lasso lazily in one paw, making figure eights in the air.

Tucka took one step forward, raised her free arm majestically and sang in a dark, worldly voice filled with sadness and regret.

> *Don't hate me because I'm beautiful,*
> *I'm rich and I'm famous too;*
> *Don't hate me because I'm beautiful,*
> *Can't you see what's true?*
> *It's not so much that you got less than me,*
> *It's just that I got more than you.*

'We love you, Tucka!' cheered someone in the balcony. The audience clapped wildly. Tucka bowed. She climbed up on to the fence, seated herself gracefully and blew kisses at her fans as the fence rolled slowly towards the front of the stage. Her spotlight came up full, and she began to speak.

'You know, girls, I get a lot of mail from people just like you. Small-town girls with small-town hopes and dreams. And not much chance of any of them ever coming true. I want you to know that I understand. That's why I'm here with you tonight. I know what you're going through. I know the person that you want to be – beautiful, successful and loved for who you really are. I know because I am that person. I wish I could make your little dreams come true. They probably won't. And maybe it's better that you just face it. But there's a silver lining in every cloud.

'True ... you can't be me, but with some expert help and with the right mix of advanced beauty products, you can certainly look a little bit more like me. And at least that would be progress.

'Listen ... there's a lot of nonsense floating around in this crazy world of ours. And the biggest bit of nonsense is this idea of "inner beauty". They say that beauty is only skin deep. But you know who says that? Ugly people. And probably because they don't even use a decent moisturizer or fur conditioner. There's just one little problem with inner beauty. Nobody can see it! So what does it get you? Nothing! I know because I was beautiful inside for years and years, and what did it get me? An invitation to my snotty cousin's twelfth birthday party, where she got every expensive present known to mouse. That's when I decided to put my beauty where it belongs. On the outside. Right on the surface. Where it can be seen and envied. Because it's a scientific fact that envy, and I mean the deep down, green kind of envy, can add unbelievable body and gloss to your fur. Better than vitamins. And look at me. I'm the living proof. Just standing here in front of you tonight and sensing how much you wish you were me is the equivalent of spending a whole week at one of my own expensive spas. Feeling envied is a wild feeling. And let me tell you, I'm feeling wild tonight!

'So let's bring out the Wild Girl Dancers and have ourselves a hoedown! Boys! Hit it!'

The banjos erupted in a galloping hop-stomp. Tucka leapt down from the fence and was joined by the Wild Girls in a whirl of calico, boots and spurs, hopping and stomping. Each one of them trying her best to stay out of the way of Tucka's high-flying kicks. The number ended with the Wild Girls hoisting Tucka on to their shoulders and balancing on their toes and tails while

151

Tucka whirled her lasso overhead and mouthed the words 'I love you!' over and over to the audience.

'I certainly don't envy them their job,' thought Hermux as the curtain slowly closed. 'Making Tucka look light as a feather ... especially the smallest one. She looked like she was having a time of it.'

The gopher announcer appeared onstage rolling a stand with a large glass fishbowl on top.

'And now, ladies and gentlemen, it's time for the grand drawing. The winner will receive a complete head-to-toe makeover to be performed tonight, live onstage, by none other than the Magician of Beauty herself, Tucka Mertslin, and her team of able assistants.'

Hermux thought this would be the perfect time for him to sneak out and look for Tucka's stateroom.

Chapter 46
ALL EARS

Hermux studied the sign that hung from the thick velvet rope.

> **PRIVATE QUARTERS**
> Public Not Permitted
> Beyond This Point

Ahead lay a short passageway. At the end of it, two louvred doors faced each other. Hermux flexed the muscles at the back of his scalp, arching and spreading his ears. He focused them on the first door and scanned it very slowly from side to side. It was dead quiet inside. He shifted his attention to the other door.

'Also empty,' he thought. 'No. That might be something.' He detected the faintest noise. Maybe a tiny rustling of some kind. He flared his ears to their utmost extension, closed his eyes and concentrated to filter out the sounds of strumming banjos that drifted up the stairs behind him. There was definitely something there. Paper. Someone inside was moving papers.

Then Hermux heard a man's voice say, 'Aha! Gotcha!'

Hermux dipped under the rope. Holding his tail carefully in

one hand and rising up on to the very tips of his toes, he crept towards the door. He pressed one eye to the louvres and peered through. Only the floor was visible. But it revealed the distinct shadow of a mouse, seated hunched over a table or desk.

Inside, Hinkum Stepfitchler looked up from the river chart he was studying and sniffed the air suspiciously. He smelled a new scent. Something vaguely unpleasant. Something with bad memories. His whiskers bristled. Then he smiled bitterly.

'Fresh-mown hay,' he thought. 'Just like summer camp. Next we'll have crickets in here singing lullabies. And mosquitoes. I hate the country! I wish I were home in Pinchester.'

Hinkum missed his mansion. He missed his study and his library. His missed his butler and his cook. He missed his extra-soft bed and his extra-big bathtub. And he missed the peace and quiet of living alone.

Tucka was beginning to get on his nerves.

There was a flurry of footsteps on the stairs. Hermux jumped back from the door. Someone was coming. He tried the other door. It was unlocked. Hermux ducked inside and scrambled furiously in the dark for somewhere to hide. He found the bed and, holding his stomach in as tightly as he could, he squirmed underneath it, yanking his tail in just as he heard the sound of a door opening.

'What a bunch of hicks!' Tucka announced. 'I've got a good mind to use real knives for the knife-throwing number.' Then the door slammed shut. Tucka continued to complain, but her voice was muffled. Hermux realized that she had gone into the other stateroom.

He squeezed out from under the bed and stationed himself with his ear against the inside of the door.

'It may be time for a change of plans, darling,' the other

mouse told Tucka. 'I think I've found what we're looking for. Look here at the map.'

Hermux strained to hear. He knew that voice.

'It's Hinkum all right!' he thought.

'I'm working on a little press release right now. We'll telegraph it out to all the papers tonight right after the show. Listen.

*** FOR IMMEDIATE RELEASE ***

Even the Queen of Beauty needs her beauty rest!

Acting under strictest doctor's orders, Tucka Mertslin announced today the cancellation of her wildly successful Wild Girls Tour. Sources close to the cosmetics tycoon turned actor-singer-dancer say that a gruelling schedule of nightly performances and nearly non-stop beauty consultations have left her in a state of complete exhaustion.

"I hope my fans will understand that I only have so much Tucka to give," she explained tearfully at her farewell performance. "And I have given it all to them."

Miss Mertslin will travel by showboat to an undisclosed location to recuperate.'

'That sounds wonderful,' Tucka answered happily. 'A real rest at last. I'm so tired of show business. So very, very tired. I had no idea it would be so crass and superficial. Could you just add a little reminder that the Wild Girl products are still available in all major department stores? You're a dear! And you're so clever! You found the library?'

'I've found a very likely spot,' Hinkum said smugly.

'And what about our other special little announcement?'

155

'Just a few more days, my dearest,' he murmured. 'It would make a nice little footnote to announcing our discovery.'

'You are a crafty one! I love that about you. Oh my goodness!' cried Tucka. 'I've got to change for the second act!'

Hermux turned from the door to run back to the bed. But what he saw caused him to let out a terrified yelp. Next to the window, dressed in ghostly white from head to toe, was Tucka herself. Hermux hit the floor and crawled for his life.

'It's Tucka!' he thought in a panic. 'She's already haunting me, and she's not even dead!'

He made it under the bed just as the door opened and the lights came on. Tucka bustled in. Hermux peeked out cautiously from under the bed ruffle. He could see the other Tucka clearly now. It was only a mannequin. An exact replica of Tucka. And it was wearing a veil and a shimmering, floor-length white wedding dress.

Tucka crooned softly to herself as she changed costumes.

Here comes the bride ...
Here comes the bride ...

Chapter 47
GETTING THE POINT

Being alone in a room with Tucka Mertslin while she changed clothes was not exactly Hermux's idea of paradise. He lay as quietly as he could. Of course, he immediately felt like sneezing. Then he got a terrible itch on his back, right under one shoulder blade. His left leg went to sleep from the knee down. And he got an awful muscle cramp in his right hip. Finally, Tucka dropped down on the bed to lace up her high-top boots and nearly knocked the breath out of him.

At last she stomped out of the stateroom and slammed the door behind her.

Hermux waited five minutes before making his escape. He was just slipping back under the velvet rope when a bony paw grabbed him by the ear and jerked him upright.

'The sign says "Private" in case you can't read!'

It was the cranky ticket-hamster. Only now he was wearing an usher's uniform.

Hermux dragged the souvenir programme from the pocket of his overalls.

'I was hoping to get Miss Mertslin's autograph for my little girl. She worships the woman! She missed the show because

157

she's home sick with spotted-fur fever. It would mean a lot to her!'

The hamster immediately released Hermux's ear and took a big step back.

'Spotted-fur fever? Never heard of it!'

'Oh yeah? It's been pretty bad around here this year. Have you had your shots?'

'No.'

'Well, you look like a healthy guy. I wouldn't worry about it. And the fur grows back eventually. Any chance of you helping me out with an autograph?'

'Catch her after the show. The stage door. Don't let me catch you sneaking around up here again!'

He escorted Hermux down the stairs, directed him back inside the darkened theatre and accompanied him all the way to his table. He motioned impatiently for Hermux to sit down.

Hermux was just about to do that when a bright spotlight swept out over the audience and focused right on him.

'Ladies and gentlemen!' crowed Tucka from the stage. 'We've got a volunteer! Blindfold him and bring him up. It's time for him to spin the Wheel of Fortune!'

'Hmmmm,' thought Hermux. 'I'd love to win a prize.' He pictured an island holiday for two. Just him and Linka. Little grass huts on a sandy beach. Or a factory tour of the Grandfather Clockworks in Burpin. A snug little bed and breakfast within walking distance of the factory. And no Turfip Dandiffer.

'Take off your hat!' Chintsy Tureen told him. She leaned close to him while she fastened the black blindfold tightly in place. 'Listen,' she said. 'Just don't move once you're on the wheel. And try to act scared. The audience loves that.'

'What do you mean?'

158

'Act scared. The knives aren't real, you ninny!'

'What knives?' asked Hermux as Chintsy led him through the audience and up on to the stage.

Someone grasped his arms and feet roughly, and he felt himself being strapped on to a wooden board. Somewhere nearby he heard the sounds of something being sharpened on a grinding wheel.

'As you can see with your own eyes, ladies and gentlemen,' blared Tucka, 'each one of these knives is sharp enough to shave a whisker. Now, spin the wheel and let's see where lady luck lands tonight!'

Chapter 48
A TURN FOR THE WORSE

Hermux began to revolve.

'Faster!' shouted Tucka. 'I'm feeling lucky tonight!'

Chintsy gave the wheel another push and Hermux felt his head and feet begin to buzz as the blood rushed to his extremities. His stomach, however, was caught in the middle. It had no place to go but over and over and over. Hermux knew he was going to be sick. Then something hit the wheel right next to his head with a resounding *thoinnggg!* A chip of wood landed in one of Hermux's ears. It tickled. But it wasn't funny. He forgot about being sick. Tucka was throwing real knives.

The next one landed nearly touching his neck. Then his shoulder. His elbow. His knee. Tucka was outlining him in razor-sharp blades.

'Stop!' Hermux managed to shout. 'Stop before you kill me!'

'That's great!' whispered Chintsy. 'The crowd's loving it! Keep screaming!'

'No! I really mean it! Stop!'

The wheel was beginning to slow. Tucka had worked her

way back up to his right elbow. The next knife sliced through the suspender of his overalls.

Hermux let out a yowl.

The audience roared.

'Only one more for a chance at the grand prize of ten thousand dollars in cash!' crowed Tucka.

'Let me off this!' Hermux yelled.

'Nonsense!' said Tucka. 'I can't let you pass up the chance of a lifetime!'

She threw the last knife with all her might. It parted the fur on Hermux's right cheek. He could feel the cold steel touching his skin.

Then the wheel jerked to a stop and the crowd groaned in disappointment.

'Looks like it's only the consolation prize!' announced Tucka cheerfully. 'Well, untie him and take off his blindfold. Then bring him over here. Pucker up, little fellow, for the kiss of your life!'

Chintsy helped Hermux down and was removing his blindfold when there was a loud commotion offstage. The side curtain parted and a glittering figure cartwheeled past, snatched the microphone from Tucka's hand and came to a stop centre stage. Chintsy couldn't believe her eyes.

It was Twitchi Tiptail. The spotlight picked her up and she started to sing in a loud bluesy voice, stamping out the slow beat with her foot and scolding the audience with one finger.

My mouse is gone,
He said he'd never leave me;
He said he'd always bring me home the cheese ...

The banjo orchestra came in on the downbeat.

Now that mouse is gone,
He done me wrong;
He said we'd dine on string beans and peas ...

'Shut up!' snapped Tucka. 'Cut that microphone! You're fired!'

But Twitchi went on singing. She crossed over to Hermux and grabbed him by the overalls, staring into his startled eyes.

Yeah, my mouse is gone (she winked),
The dirty rat!
He lied and he deceived me,
He locked my heart and threw away the keys!

And with that, she turned Hermux around. 'Get out of here!' she whispered. Then she booted him off the stage and into the audience.

The crowd went wild.

So did Tucka. She raced over to the Wheel of Fortune and pulled off a knife.

'Look out, Twitchi!' cried Chintsy.

Tucka took aim. Twitchi ducked.

And that is when Birch stood up in the balcony and shouted, like only a chipmunk in danger can shout, 'Fire! Everybody run for your life!'

Chapter 49
WESTWARD HO!

Birch sneezed.

'There's another blanket back there,' Linka called to him over the sound of the engine. 'Wrap up well until we get it warmed up in here.' She gave the gauges a final check and then increased the throttle and turned the plane into the wind.

'It will serve me right if I catch a cold,' said Birch grumpily. 'It was a stupid thing to do. But I saw Tucka getting ready to throw that knife, and I just plain panicked.'

'Don't worry!' said Hermux. 'Nobody got hurt. A lot of people thought it was just part of the show. Until the fire sprinklers went on. And it sure got us off the boat in a hurry.'

'Besides,' said Linka, 'I needed to take a shower to get all that make-up off.'

Hermux stole a look at her as the plane gathered speed down the bumpy runway. The lights of the instrument panel cast a dull green glow on her damp fur. Even matted and dishevelled, she looked lovely to him.

With a rush and a roar, the plane lifted off into the velvety night.

'I hope we didn't get Chintsy and the girls fired,' said Linka as they gained altitude. 'They were awfully decent to me.'

'Tucka was already planning to fire them all tomorrow,' said Hermux. He described the discussion that he had overheard in Hinkum's cabin.

'Did you find out where they are heading?' asked Linka.

'No,' said Hermux, disappointed.

'Well, I did,' announced Birch proudly. 'Got up to the pilot house during intermission and had a nice visit with the captain. Pleasant young fellow. More than happy to show an old farmer his charts. Even showed me where he was laying out a course up the Longish River. All the way to Dead Rat Falls. He'd just got the orders from below. They leave tomorrow at dawn.'

'Dead Rat Falls doesn't sound like a very nice place for a honeymoon,' said Hermux.

'What do you mean?' asked Linka, somewhat startled.

'Tucka and Hinkum. They're getting married. Her wedding dress is all ready. I think the statue of the cat king is going to be her wedding present.'

'Why, that scoundrel!' said Birch. 'It's not his to give away. We've got to find it first. Linka, how much longer can you fly tonight?'

'We've got a full tank of fuel. And I couldn't sleep if I had to. I'm much too revved up. There's nowhere I'd rather be right now than in this plane.'

'Then let's head west,' said Birch. 'There are a lot of places along the Longish where we can land. Tomorrow we'll continue on to Dead Rat Falls and start looking there.'

Linka circled the plane around and set a course due west.

Hermux looked back towards the lights of Boomerville. The big neon lips between the smokestacks of the SS *Beauty Queen* smiled ruby red, blinked, smiled again and went dark.

'Well,' he said. 'At least we gave the people of Boomerville something to talk about until the next pea harvest.'

Chapter 50
AROUND AND AROUND

Hermux clung to the saddle as the grasshopper soared into the night air. Ahead of him flew Linka on the luminous back of a firefly. Ahead of her rode Tucka on a plump ladybird. Tucka spurred her mount viciously. 'Move it!' she commanded. Hermux gasped when he recognized Terfle's familiar black spots.

'Leave her alone!' he cried, horrified.

The crack of the whip was Tucka's only answer.

Hermux urged his grasshopper to fly faster. But Tucka remained out of reach as around and around they flew. Then with sudden relief Hermux realized they were riding on a carousel. Hinkum was there too, riding on a shiny black stinkbug. And Birch on an iridescent dragonfly.

At the centre of the carousel a mechanical banjo orchestra plunked away at a zigzag waltz, slightly out of tune. Next to the carousel sat a monumental gold statue of a cat. On its head was a gleaming crown of jewels. In its mouth it held a golden ring. On the ring was a gigantic diamond that sparkled and glowed as if it were on fire.

Each of the riders reached for the ring as they spun by it. On his third try, Hermux nearly got it. But of course, it was Tucka who wrapped her tail around the pommel of her saddle, leaned out, swung about wildly and snatched the ring right out of the cat's mouth.

'I've got it!' she shouted. But then there was an awful roar. The cat came to life in a fury and raked the carousel with its giant claws. Then it grabbed Linka in its jaws. She let out a horrible scream. Hermux wanted to help her, but he couldn't move. His arms and legs were pinned to his sides.

That's when he woke up and found himself twisted into a tangle in his own sleeping bag. He fought his way out and sat up. They had slept beneath the plane right where Linka had set it down on the broad, flat bank of the Longish River. Linka's sleeping bag was neatly rolled and tied. Birch was still snoring away.

It was a beautiful, clear morning. Hermux sniffed eagerly. The air was cool and sharp with the scent of something pungent and spicy. It was coffee! He scrambled out of his pyjamas and into his ice-cold overalls.

Linka had gathered driftwood and built a fire away from the plane. She sat there at a tiny desk, writing as he walked up.

'Good morning,' he said politely.

Linka looked up from her notebook and smiled. Her fur looked clean and silky again. She had brushed it back simply on her face. She looked wonderful.

'There's fresh coffee,' she said, getting up from her camp stool. 'And there's a nice little beach right down there. The water's a little brisk, but it feels good. I'm just finishing up my flight log. I should have done it when we landed, but I was beat.'

Hermux examined her desk in amazement. It was a wooden box on wheels. Its side opened out to make the desk. The box itself was divided into small compartments, each of them carefully labelled.

'Coffeepot, matches, coffee, cups, plates, bowls, utensils, paper, pens, notebooks,' read Hermux.

'What do you think?' she asked him. 'It's my camp kitchen-office. I built it myself. Cups are right there. Watch out for the coffeepot. It's hot.'

'It's beautiful!' Hermux said admiringly. 'Everything is so organized.' He took a cup.

'I can't stand not finding things when I need them,' Linka explained. 'I've got another one for tools.'

'Oh! I'd like to see that. I've always dreamed of having a little watchmaker's bench that I could travel with. You know ... go interesting places and work while I'm there.'

'Of course I know,' she said. 'That's what I do. Or what I did. I'm not sure what I do now.'

Hermux took in the broad river, the expanse of open, empty sky overhead and the chiselled hills that loomed to the west. He listened to the silence around them. Except for the crackle of the fire, there was no sound at all. Not the river. No wind. No birds. It was a very lonely place.

'Won't you miss this?' he asked her.

'I don't know how I'm going to do it,' she said rather hopelessly. 'It seems impossible.' Then she brightened. 'But I'll manage. I've done impossible things before. And Turfip is being very patient. Of course, he may have a thing or two to say about it when he comes back and finds me gone. But we'll cross that bridge when we come to it. Now, have some coffee. I'm going to wake Birch and take a look at the plane.'

Hermux poured his coffee. Then he retrieved his journal from his pack and sat down at Linka's desk. It was just the right size. Sitting in the fresh air by the warmth of the fire was very

pleasant. He sipped his coffee and thought about the dream he'd
had. Then he opened his journal.

Thank you for daylight. For being able to see things
like they really are. Thank you for maps and compasses and
rulers. Thank you for tables and coffeepots. And motors.
And notebooks and pens. And if there really is a golden cat
mummy out there somewhere in the desert, please just let
it stay dead.

And please, I know that Mirrin will take excellent care of
her, but please keep an eye on Terfle while I'm gone. Don't let
her get too lonely.

Chapter 51
PLANNING COMMITTEE

'I suggest we start by making a list of what needs to be done,' announced Linka as she poured her second cup of coffee. She opened her notebook and wrote in the date and THINGS TO DO in bold block letters.

Birch nodded. 'Excellent idea. The first thing is to find a permanent place to camp near Dead Rat Falls. We need to be able to see the river without being seen.'

'We need a good place to land and take off,' said Linka.

'We need water,' said Hermux.

'We need shade,' said Birch.

'We need to figure out when Hinkum and Tucka will arrive as accurately as we can,' said Hermux. 'If we're going to use the plane to look for the canyon, we'd better get it done before they get here.'

Linka added, 'We need to set aside a fuel reserve to get us back to civilization. That will also determine how much time we can spend in the air. Birch, where's the nearest town with an airstrip?'

'Hmmmn. Well, there's Paydirt. That's where the Shady flows into the Longish.'

'Right,' said Linka with frown. 'Paydirt. I was there once. It's a pretty rough town. They watered my fuel. That's not something you forget. I think we'd be better off going back to Boomerville unless it's a real emergency. At least the people there are honest.'

'OK. And I want to lay out the map in a grid before we start searching,' said Birch. 'We haven't got much time, so we'd better use it wisely.'

'I want to take a better look at the bronze gear you found,' Hermux told Birch. 'I only saw it very briefly. Maybe there's some kind of clue there.'

'Anything else?' asked Linka.

'That's all I can think of for now,' said Hermux.

'Then let's pack up and get going,' said Birch. 'I'll get the gear out for Hermux. And I'll work on the map in the plane.'

Chapter 52
THE COURSE OF LEAST RESISTANCE

As they flew north, Hermux watched the river valley below. It grew narrower and narrower, and the land on each side rose higher and higher. To the west honey-gold sand stretched all the way to the horizon. There was no sign of a road or a house anywhere.

'Looks pretty lonely, doesn't it?' said Hermux, shielding his eyes from the glare of the late afternoon sun.

'Worse than lonely,' said Linka. 'But beautiful in its way. Birch, did you actually live in the desert?'

'Only on the edges. The canyon country. I never went too far into the sand. Too hot in the daytime. And too dangerous at night.'

'Dangerous how?' asked Hermux.

'Nasty things that bite and sting.'

'Oh,' said Hermux. 'That's something to look forward to.' Hermux looked back at the ocean of sand with increased respect and a touch of apprehension.

The walls of the canyon seemed to be all that were holding it back. And those walls were breached and broken in a thousand places by deep cracks. Hundreds of them were canyons in their own right. Through each crack flowed the sand – dropped by storms, blown by wind. It trickled. It sifted. It drifted. By gully and by wash it flowed to the river. And from there it was swept downstream, endlessly shifting its shape in channels and bars all the way to the river's delta, a thousand miles south in the Gulf of Tretch.

'So the library is in one of these canyons?' asked Hermux.

'That's what I'm hoping,' said Birch.

'But which one? Didn't you already look here?'

'I did. And I didn't find it. But this time I've got a big advantage.'

'What?'

'I'm getting to see it from the air,' said Birch in a tone of awestruck wonder. Then he added, 'And the two of you are with me.'

'Look up there,' Linka said. 'See that cloud? It's mist. I think we're getting close to Dead Rat Falls.'

The Longish River begins as a tiny ribbon of snowmelt high in the Lop-eared Mountains. Dropping down through the rain-soaked highlands, it grows deeper and faster as the waters of a hundred other streams join the headlong rush towards the upper cataract of Crookpaw Falls. Below the thundering falls, the river coils into itself, forming an enormous lake. There it gathers strength for the long crossing of the Great Desert. Through five hundred miles of barren sand it weaves a narrow ribbon of life. Then, leaving the desert behind, it plunges a hundred metres over the sandstone cliffs at Dead Rat Falls. It was here, more than a century ago, that an unlucky band of trade rats met their tragic end attempting to establish an overland route to the rich mushroom forests of the Northwest Territory. In their exhaustion they misjudged the strength of the river current and were swept to their deaths. Since then, very few rodents of any kind had dared to venture above Dead Rat Falls.

'Circle around and let's look for a place to land above the falls,' Birch suggested. 'We'll be able to watch for Tucka and Hinkum. And they won't be able to see us.'

Chapter 53
TIME IS OF THE ESSENCE

The thunder of the falls could be heard clearly now over the sound of the plane's engine. As they got closer, the air above the canyon seemed to vibrate with the force of the water.

In his entire life Hermux had never seen anything like Dead Rat Falls. Without thinking, he grabbed Linka's paw. 'Oh, I'm sorry!' he said, letting go. 'But look at all that water! Birch! Would you look at that! It's the most amazing thing I've ever seen!' Hermux was so excited that his ears felt hot and itchy. 'Look at all that water! Just pounding down there!'

The plane began to rock.

'Everybody hold on,' Linka cautioned. 'It's going to get a little choppy with the updraught.'

She brought them around above the falls, and then came in low over the east side and followed the rim of the escarpment south again. On the west side, the sand dunes came right up to the edge of the canyon and spilled over. On the east rim the sand gave way to thickets of cactus and greasewood and then disappeared altogether into rolling hills of scrubby grass.

Linka motioned towards a narrow meadow. 'I think I could

put her down there,' she said. 'There's plenty of room and the ground looks level.'

'It looks good to me,' Birch said. 'Let's do it!'

Linka made one flyover to be sure and then brought them in for a smooth landing.

'If you two gather some firewood,' she said, 'I'll get the kitchen unpacked, and we'll have dinner made before it gets dark.'

An hour later the tidy camp was made.

'This is the life,' said Hermux, inhaling the very pleasant smell of onions roasting with carrots. Linka was at work at her desk.

'According to my figures,' she said, 'Tucka and Hinkum could be here as early as tomorrow at noon. If they push it. And knowing Tucka, they will.'

'That gives us the morning to use the plane,' said Birch. 'I'd like to take a good look around before they get here. It's our only chance.' He unfolded Mirrin's copy of the map. 'Here is what we're looking for. A canyon with plum-coloured walls. The entrance to the library is at the back of the canyon.'

'It's not much to go on, is it?' said Hermux. 'And what about this? Do you have any idea what it is?' He held up the bronze gear that Birch had found with the scroll.

'Only that it has something to do with "the wheels of time" and "the King's Delight". It may be some way of bringing him back to life.'

'You mean like a seance? That sounds creepy,' said Linka. 'What could it be?'

'I honestly have no idea,' Birch admitted. 'I was hoping that Hermux could tell us.'

Hermux laid the gear in the lantern light on Linka's desk. It was as big as a plate.

'It looks to me like the wheel of a dead escapement,' he said.

Linka gasped, 'So it can bring people back to life?'

'No. No. It's part of a clock. A dead escapement is a mechanism for driving a pendulum. It was an important breakthrough in clock-making about two hundred years ago. But they were never made of bronze. It's too brittle. See? One of the teeth has broken off. And some of the others are chipped. It's hard to believe, but apparently someone, or something, was making pendulum clocks thousands of years before we even invented the sundial. What I want to know is how they powered them. Wind-up springs? Weights? Or did they do something different?' He pointed towards the falls. 'With all the drop here, maybe they were using water power.'

Linka lifted the escape wheel and examined it. 'It's quite heavy, isn't it?' she said.

'And big. The clock itself must have been as big as the tower clock at Gurfenville.' Hermux couldn't help admiring Linka's paws as she held the bronze wheel. They were nimble and confident with clean, short-clipped claws. But on her ring finger a brilliant twinkle of silver reminded him that she belonged to someone else. Hermux sighed.

'Time is so mysterious, isn't it?' Linka asked. 'This must be very exciting for you.'

'Yes,' said Hermux wearily. 'Very exciting. And a little confusing too.'

'What do you mean?'

'Oh. Just trying to fit the pieces together. They don't seem to go where I want them to.'

'But that's one of the things I like most about adventure. It's full of surprises.'

After dinner, Linka sliced a pear and set it out with a piece of crumbly Lankimmer cheese. Then she opened her flight log and began to make the day's entries. Birch settled down to mark off his map in a carefully drawn grid.

Hermux nibbled his pear and cheese. Then he got out his journal and walked away from the camp. He crossed the meadow and picked his way through the brush to the edge of the canyon. He climbed up on a boulder and gazed out at the vast emptiness. In the moonlight the falls hung like a curtain of white noise over the black cliffs. Above and behind them the sands stood guard – motionless, silent and eternal.

Thank you for maps and compasses. Thank you for winding rivers and crashing waterfalls. For empty canyons and rising moons. For campfires and carrots. And for some time to get to know Linka better.

By the way, thank you for time in general. I wonder what time is exactly and where it comes from. I've never really considered it before. And where does it go? I wonder how much time I have. Have I spent it wisely? Or have I wasted it?

I wonder what the king's 'wheels of time' were. Was it only a clock? Does that mean that time was the 'King's Delight'? Or was it something else? Something that I'd rather not know about? Something unpleasant that would be better left in the dark.

Are we doing the right thing to bring it to light? I wonder...

'Do you mind if I join you?'

Hermux hadn't heard Linka approach. He closed his journal quickly.

178

'Please,' he said. 'Climb up. I'm just sitting here enjoying the evening.'

'It's beautiful here, isn't it?' Linka said, sitting down beside him. 'It seems so peaceful. Even the sound of the falls. It's like time is slowed down.'

'I was just thinking about time.'

'You must think about it a lot.'

'No. Actually, I'm afraid I've hardly ever given it much thought. I'm always trying to fix it. But I realize tonight that I hardly know what it is. I'm a watchmaker, and time is a mystery to me.'

'That doesn't sound so bad. I've been almost everywhere. And the world is still a mystery to me.'

'I was just thinking about that too.'

'What?'

'Mystery.'

'What do you mean?'

'Well, what we're looking for is a mystery. We don't know if we'll find it. And when we do, we're not sure if we'll like what we find. We might be better off to leave it in the dark. The "King's Delight" may not be so delightful to us.'

'I see. Or rather I don't see. Which is what you're saying. We're searching for something we've never seen. And we won't know until we see it whether it was worth the search. But that's what adventure is. Finding out for yourself. That's why I'm an adventuress. Or why I was. Oh!' she said, suddenly very unhappy.

'Will you really have to give it up?' asked Hermux. 'I can't believe that.'

Linka covered her face with her paws and sobbed.

'I was noticing your ring earlier,' said Hermux, hoping to cheer her up. 'It's very beautiful. Is that your engagement ring?'

'Oh, no. I left my engagement ring at home,' she said, wiping her eyes.

'I see,' said Hermux. His left ear twitched.

'Turfip insisted on a diamond. It's not the right ring for adventure. So I wore this. I designed it myself.'

She took it off and handed it to Hermux. He looked at it curiously. It had a thick hoop and a broad, flat bezel engraved with the image of an aeroplane.

'It's an unusual design. Is it a seal?'

'You might say that. As a matter of fact, it was inspired by our first adventure.'

'You and Turfip?'

'No. You and me,' she said.

'Our first adventure?'

'Look!' She grabbed Hermux's arm and squeezed it hard. She pointed above the falls. 'Shooting stars! Make a wish!'

And Hermux did. But he didn't have much hope that it would ever come true.

Chapter 54
LAYER UPON LAYER

'Wake up, Hermux!' said Birch. 'We've got a big day ahead of us! We can't afford to waste any time.'

Hermux opened his eyes and then shut them again. It was still dark. 'What time is it?' he asked, somewhat crankily.

'Close to seven. The sun's just coming up!'

'Why so early? Shouldn't we be saving up our strength?'

'We have saved it. Now we're going to use it.'

'Hermux!' called Linka from the campfire. 'Come on! There's coffee!'

It was freezing outside the sleeping bag. Hermux left his pyjamas on and dressed right over them. He shook his shoes out the way Birch had shown him and carefully looked inside each one before he put them on. Then he ran for the fire.

'Now I wish I had bought a tail-warmer,' he thought, remembering the soft cashmere tubes with the little pastel pompoms that he'd seen at Orsik & Arrbale. 'And they were on sale too.' He poured himself a cup of coffee and then tried to arrange his tail to catch some of the heat from the fire.

'So, what's the plan?' he asked.

'Birch and I are going to take the plane up. We'll start on this side about five miles south. Then we'll make our way up to the falls and start down the west rim. We're betting that if there is anything to find, it will be on this side, where there's water and vegetation.'

'And what do I do?'

'You stay here,' explained Birch. 'Take the binoculars and look around for any sign of the canyon. Plum-coloured. It ought to stand out in all the orange and red. You've got a great view from this height. Concentrate on the west side of the river.'

'Right,' said Hermux. 'The west side of the river, where there are no signs of life or anything. Maybe this afternoon I could go up with Linka and you could use the binoculars.'

'This morning is all we've got,' said Birch. 'Once Tucka and Hinkum are here, we'll have to be careful using the plane.'

An hour later Linka and Birch were airborne. Hermux found a rock ledge that jutted out over the canyon. It gave him a panoramic view of the falls and the cliffs and canyons on the opposite side.

'I'll start at the falls and work south from there,' thought Hermux. In the bright morning light the canyon looked like it had been sliced from a thousand-layered lemon and orange sherbet cake. It looked delicious. Hermux couldn't help thinking that if he were still at home, he would be just dropping into Lanayda's for his morning doughnut. She made a wonderful lemon doughnut with crunchy little bits of candied lemon rind. But then, of course, if he were at home, he wouldn't be in the middle of an adventure with Linka Perflinger, who had, if he had heard her correctly last night, designed a special ring to remember their first adventure together.

Hermux sighed and focused the binoculars. The first break in the canyon wall was a narrow gorge about a quarter of a mile south of the falls. He studied the striations of the stone, starting at the bottom and working slowly up to the rim. Reds, yellows, oranges, golds, browns and greys. No plum. It made him a little dizzy.

There was another, larger gorge just beyond that. The same colours. Then another and another. Then he shifted his position, walking south along the rim to a new vantage point. There the river began to widen and the walls of the canyon became more irregular. The gorges grew larger. They became canyons. But nothing out of the ordinary appeared. An hour later he moved south again. He was beginning to understand the structure of the stone. The layers of sandstone and shale. The occasional up-thrusts of basalt. The free-standing mesas. But he was also beginning to feel discouraged. There were just too many canyons. And they all looked the same.

That's when he noticed the patch.

He wasn't sure if it was the slight shift in colour or the way that the lines and layers didn't quite line up. But there was some-thing definitely odd about a section of rock about twenty metres wide and more than thirty metres tall. It looked as though some-one had built a massive stone wall across the entrance of a small canyon.

Hermux put down the binoculars. 'I must be seeing things. The glare and the stripes are getting to me.' He took a drink from his canteen and rested his eyes. Then he looked again, fo-cusing the binoculars very carefully and scanning the rock metre by metre. He couldn't tell if he were imagining it or not, but he seemed to detect a certain regularity in the surface. As though it had been cut into rough blocks and then stacked. He studied the area between the rock face and the river. It was about a half a mile to the edge of the water. He could just make out the impression of an old streambed that began at the river and ended at the rock wall. He tried to look over the wall, if it was a wall. What lay beyond was obscured in shadows. But the shadows had a distinctly purple tinge.

Hermux made careful note of the location – a mile and a half south of the falls on the west side of the canyon. Then he started back to camp as fast as he could walk.

Chapter 55
OVER THE TOP

The wind from the propeller stuck his fur flat to his face.

'I found something!' Hermux shouted, clambering up on to the wing of the plane as it rolled to a stop. 'I think I found the canyon! Well, not exactly the canyon. But a wall. I think it's in front of the canyon!'

Linka cut the engine.

'We saw you signalling with the mirror,' she said. 'We were afraid you were hurt.'

'No, not hurt! Just excited! I needed to tell you. There's a wall! The same rock, but the colours are different. Just a little! And the lines don't match. Well, they match, but not quite. And there's an old riverbed, but it's all filled in with silt. And it looks plum-coloured or at least purplish from here. But it's all shadowed, so I couldn't tell exactly!'

Birch climbed out of the plane. 'Calm down, Hermux! Calm down! Just tell us what you saw. Tell us exactly what you saw.'

So he did. As soon as Linka and Birch heard the details, they wanted a closer look.

Linka checked her watch. It was already ten-thirty. 'Let's go right now. If this is it, and we can find a place to land, we'll have just enough time to move camp before we have to worry about Tucka.'

Minutes later they were in the air with Hermux guiding the way. Linka took the plane straight down into the main canyon, skimming across the surface of the river past the small gorges and the mouths of the side canyons.

Then he spotted it. 'That's it!' he announced triumphantly. He tapped the windshield. 'Right there. See the way the colour changes? It's not real. It's just rocks.'

'The whole canyon is rocks, Hermux,' said Linka. She couldn't hide the fact that she had expected a little more. 'What do you think, Birch?'

'Well, let's go up and take a look. I can't tell anything from this.'

As Linka banked out over the river and climbed, Hermux pointed down at the ground.

'See,' he said somewhat lamely. 'There's an impression there. It's like an old streambed that leads right to the wall. It used to be a canyon.'

Neither Linka nor Birch said a word.

Then the plane soared over the lip of stone.

'Oh my gosh!' cried Linka. Behind the towering wall, which was some three metres thick, was a narrow canyon. It cut deep into the escarpment, and its dark walls were the colour of a ripe plum.

'You did it!' shouted Birch. He slapped Hermux on the shoulder. He tousled the fur on his head. He thumped the back of the seat with his feet. He let out a whoop. 'Land! Land! Take her down! We found it!'

Chapter 56
CARVED IN STONE

'Everybody be quiet!' Linka said tersely. 'I don't have much room to manoeuvre, and I need to concentrate.'

The canyon opened out slightly and curved to the north for about half a mile. Then, as abruptly as it began, it ended in a sheer cliff that rose straight up to meet the dunes above. The canyon was completely empty. Linka pulled back on the stick and brought the plane into a steep climb.

'Did you see anything?' Hermux asked.

'No,' said Linka. 'Birch? Any idea what we're looking for?'

'Just find a place to land!' he said.

'Oh, sure!' said Linka, bringing the plane back around and down for another pass. 'A place to land. In a dead-end canyon. No problem!' She checked her watch. 'All right. Hold on! I'm taking her down.'

Hermux felt his breakfast shift violently as the floor of the canyon came up to meet the plane. Then Linka lowered the flaps. The plane touched down to a smooth landing on the hard packed sand. She cut the engines and looked at her watch. 'Look fast,' she told Birch. 'They could be steaming up to the falls at any minute.'

They clambered down from the plane. Inside the canyon it was dead silent.

'This is weird,' said Hermux. 'I've never heard anything this quiet before. You can't even hear the falls. Hello!' he shouted. 'Anybody here?'

'Hermux, nobody's going to be here after three thousand years.'

'You're right. I was just checking. Birch! What do we do now? I don't see anything!'

'OK,' Birch said. 'Let's just take a minute and look around carefully. We saw how the entrance to the canyon was concealed. Let's start with the walls here. See if we see anything out of the ordinary. It could be anything ... even something as simple as that bunch of *Typha latifolia* carved in the rock over there.' He gestured casually with one paw towards the base of the cliff. Then his tail stiffened. His eyes rolled back in his head and his teeth made a peculiar chattering noise.

'What is it?' asked Hermux.

'It's a carving!' said Linka. 'Something's carved there in the stone!'

Hermux suddenly saw it. 'Are they sausages?' he asked.

'No!' Linka said. 'Not sausages. *Typha latifolia!* They're reed mace!'

'What's reed mace?'

'They're CATTAILS!' said Birch, recovering his senses. 'It's the top of a giant column shaped like a bundle of cattails. There's a whole row of them carved into the cliff. They're buried in the sand.' He ran forward and began digging frantically.

Linka pulled him away.

'Birch, we've got to get out of here. Let's go back and get our stuff before the showboat arrives. Then we'll come back here and set up camp. We need our tools and supplies. If we move fast, we can stay ahead of them. We don't know if Hinkum has the exact location yet. And he's still got to find a way around the stone wall. Unless he knows some way to get through it.'

Chapter 57
NICE DIGS

To avoid being seen, Linka took the long way on the flight back to their camp. She flew out into the desert and skirted the rim of the canyon, staying well below the sight lines of the river below.

They broke camp without even stopping to eat lunch. They worked quickly and quietly, rolling sleeping bags, folding tents, repacking the kitchen box and loading it all into the plane. Then, as stealthily as they had come, they retraced their route back to the hidden canyon.

The flight back seemed to take forever. Our three adventurers were so excited about what they were about to do that they couldn't speak. Linka's landing was not nearly so smooth this time. It might have been the added weight of the gear. Or maybe she was just the tiniest bit distracted by the idea of discovering a lost civilization. It didn't really matter. They hardly noticed the bumps and skids.

As the plane came to a stop in the perfect stillness of the canyon, they all started talking at once.

'Let's start digging!' said Birch.

'Let's set up camp!' said Linka.

'Let's eat lunch!' said Hermux.

They all laughed.

'Well, if you two would excuse me,' Birch said very politely, 'I would really like to start digging right away.'

'Sure, Birch,' said Linka. 'We've still got a few hours of light. You get started on the digging. I'll do camp. Then I want to take a look around. Some fresh water would be nice.'

'And I'll make lunch!' said Hermux. 'And after that, if you wouldn't mind, I would like just the littlest, tiniest bit of a nap. Then I'll be good as new, and I'll help Birch with the digging.'

★ ★ ★

An hour and a half later Hermux woke up. It was pleasantly warm in the tent, and even more pleasantly warm inside the sleeping bag. He rubbed his eyes and sat up and stretched. It was time to get to work.

Outside there was no sign of Linka or Birch. Hermux got a shovel and walked up the hill towards the cliff where they'd found the cattail carvings. As he got closer, he heard whistling. It must be Birch.

When he reached the edge of the hole that Birch had excavated, Hermux whistled too.

The cattail columns had grown considerably. A row of them now rose gracefully up the smooth surface of the stone. In the centre the tip of Birch's tail was barely visible above a spray of sand.

'Birch!' called Hermux. 'It's amazing! How did you do it?'

'Hermux, come here and look at this!'

Hermux half-skittered and half-slid down the side of the sandy crater.

'What is it?'

191

'What do you think?' asked Birch. He stopped digging and stepped back from the rock wall. Hermux could see a dull green surface set into the stone.

'It looks like bronze,' said Hermux.

'It is bronze.'

'It's a door!' said Hermux. 'It's the top of a door.'

'It's the top of a pair of doors,' said Birch in a careful voice. 'Massive doors set in the side of a mountain.'

Hermux looked at Birch. He had sand all over him. It covered his one good ear. It was stuck in his eyebrows. It was caked on his nose and flecked on his lips. It sifted from his whiskers as he spoke. His overalls were torn and stained. His left paw was cut and bleeding. He was hoarse and out of breath. And frankly, thought Hermux with a sniff, he could use a bath in a big way.

But seeing him there, trembling with excitement at what they had found, Hermux finally understood why Mirrin loved him.

'You really did it, Birch. You found it.'

'No, Hermux. We found it.'

'Well, where should I dig?' asked Hermux. As he spoke, a cascade of sand flowed back and buried the bronze door again.

'We've got to start moving the sand out of here, away from the excavation. Do you think you could carry sand for a while?'

'Sure. I'll get some buckets. I'm probably better at carrying than digging. Anyway, how long could it take?'

★ ★ ★

Three hours later Hermux announced, 'I'm exhausted, and I've hardly made a dent. I've got to take a break. I didn't know there was this much sand on the whole earth.'

Birch kept right on digging. Hermux sat down behind him and studied the bronze doors, which now stood more than a full storey tall. Centred at the top of the doors, an image of the sun stood out in relief. Rays of light descended from it towards an undulating horizon line that spanned both doors.

'How big do you think the doors are?' asked Hermux.

'I can't tell yet,' said Birch. 'Big enough for a cat, I guess.'

'Just how big were cats?'

'No idea.'

'But you're sure they're dead! Right? I mean, if there ever were any cats inside this, they'd be dead by now. Wouldn't they? They didn't look too friendly in Mirrin's paintings.'

'Well, if it's a tomb, then I think we could confidently say that they'd probably be dead. A long time ago.'

The sun had left the canyon, and it was beginning to cool.

'Should I go and look for Linka? It's been quite a while. I'm starting to worry a little,' said Hermux.

'She's OK. I'd be more worried about you, if you didn't come back.'

A loud cry broke the silence in the canyon.

'Yoo-hoo!'

Hermux scrambled up to the top of the dig, but he couldn't see anyone.

'Up here!'

He looked up the side of the canyon. There was Linka, standing about thirty metres up. She waved. He waved back. Then he watched in amazement as she began to walk down the wall of the cliff – effortlessly as though she were descending a flight of stairs cut into the face of the rock. Which she was, as he discovered when he ran to meet her.

'Look, I found these stairs that go all the way up,' she said cheerfully. 'And water. There's a little spring halfway up. It looks like there was a big cistern on top. Cut right into the rock. But it's filled up with sand. And I spotted the showboat. They're tied up below the falls.'

She tapped the binoculars that hung from her neck. 'I watched them getting ready to unload a four-wheel-drive truck off the boat. And they're building some sort of giant crate. Do you think that's for the mummy? Could Hinkum know another way into the canyon? Anyway, I don't think we've got much time. What's happening here?'

Chapter 58
CLOSED UNTIL FURTHER NOTICE

Hermux and Linka carted away sand as Birch continued to dig. Slowly more and more of the doors came into view, and the image continued to take shape. The rolling horizon line became distant hills. A river flowed from the hills. It became a waterfall. Its banks became a canyon. Its waters grew broad and smooth.

'It's the Longish River,' said Hermux. 'It must be!'

'There's something here!' said Birch, kicking up a new flurry of sand. 'Doorknobs!'

Then he stopped digging. He stood up slowly, wincing with the effort of straightening his lower back. He brushed off his face. 'And there's a lock,' he said, disappointed.

'Let me see it,' said Linka, sliding down to where Birch was working. 'I'm pretty good with a hairpin.'

'It will take an awfully big hairpin,' said Birch. Hermux gave him a hand climbing out of the excavation. The day had been a long one, and the excitement of the find was beginning to wear off. He was plainly tired and discouraged.

'It's nearly dark,' said Hermux. 'Why don't we eat dinner and turn in early? Then we'll get a fresh start in the morning.'

'I've found something,' said Linka. 'It looks like a piece of scroll.'

Hermux and Birch scrambled back down to where she was digging. As her paws swept the sand away, a yellowed sheet of parchment came into view. Two faint rows of symbols filled its surface.

Birch kneeled over it and studied it in the dying light.

'What does it say?' asked Hermux.

For a moment Birch was lost in thought. He seemed far, far away. Then he clapped his paw to his forehead and began to laugh.

'What?' demanded Linka.

'It's a note!' giggled Birch.

'To whom?' asked Hermux.

'To us!'

'Who's it from?' asked Linka.

'It's from the librarian,' said Birch. He pointed to each symbol as he read the note. '"Library closed for repairs. Will be back shortly." He must have written it before he went to town to get the gear fixed.'

'Well, that was nice of him,' said Hermux. 'Does it say where he put the key?'

Chapter 59
GETTING BELOW THE SURFACE

Hermux sipped his coffee and watched the morning sunlight creep down the face of the cliff above the bronze doors. It felt good to be alive. Despite his sore shoulders and back, he was looking forward to getting started on the dig. Besides, it was a very important day. Not just for him and Birch and Linka. It was important for everyone. 'It might change the course of history,' he thought. 'It might change everything – who we are and where we come from. What's possible. And not possible. We'd have to rethink everything.'

He shivered a little at the idea. Hermux liked things just so – neat, organized and orderly. Like clockwork. That's what he loved about being a watchmaker. It was predictable. Like history. To Hermux, history had always seemed like a giant clock. It got wound up and then it ran very smoothly, one thing leading to the next. You knew when things started, and you knew when they ended. And they always happened in the same order. You could count on that. Now if it turned out that the order had been wrong all along, history would fall apart. Hermux, who did not like messes in any shape or form, found himself helping to make a mess out of history.

He felt a little guilty.

'But then,' he thought, 'messes get straightened out. It will just mean putting the pieces back together. And I've always liked a good puzzle. Speaking of which, how are we ever going to get those doors unlocked?'

The sun was hitting them now, lighting up the river scene. Hermux went over for a closer look. He stared up at the massive shapes. He kicked one tentatively. It was as solid as the cliff. He examined the door frame cut into the rock. The door fitted it perfectly. Not enough space to slide a knife in, much less a crowbar. And it would take a crowbar as big as a tree to make a dent in these doors.

'Where would you hide a key?' he said to himself. 'Under a flowerpot. And where would you put a flowerpot? Beside the door.' He started digging at the door frame, half hoping and half expecting a flowerpot to miraculously appear.

It didn't.

But what did appear about half a metre down was a small bronze plaque attached to the door frame.

An arrow pointed away from the doors. Below it were two symbols.

One was a mouse.

The other was a door.

Chapter 60
OPEN DOOR POLICY

Birch arrived at a run, his toothbrush clutched in one paw. Linka was right behind him.

'Are you hurt?' she panted. 'That was an awful scream!'

'I meant to sound excited!'

'Well, you did!'

'I found something! A sign!' Hermux said proudly, pointing at the plaque. 'And I can read Cat. At least simple Cat. It says "mouse door this way". Doesn't it?'

Birch ran his paw over the worn bronze. 'Not quite,' he said. 'You've got the gist of it. But you missed something.'

'What?'

'This mouse is wearing a collar,' said Birch. He wiped a smear of toothpaste from the short hairs of his muzzle.

'So, what does that mean?'

'It means that "mouse door" is a little vague. "Service entrance" is more like it.'

'Service entrance?' said Hermux. 'You think mice were servants? To cats?'

'If they were lucky.'

'That's awful!' said Hermux.

'Let's worry about that later,' interrupted Linka. 'Right now we don't have time. Let's dig for the service entrance. If it's built for mice, we ought to be able to figure out how to open it. How are your paws, Birch? You want us to dig or carry?'

'I'll dig,' said Birch. 'It can't be far.'

And it wasn't. Following the direction of the arrow, Birch began a trench along the rock wall away from the doors. In less than an hour, the upper frame of a door was visible.

Sand flew everywhere as Birch attacked the digging with renewed energy. Hermux and Linka formed a short bucket brigade up and away from the trench, swinging, heaving and dumping as fast as they could to keep up with him. Luckily for them it was such a small door, even by mouse standards, that it didn't take long to clear away a space in front of it.

'All right,' said Birch. 'We're there! Let's break it down! Do we have anything to use as a battering ram?'

'Could we take a short break before we batter anything?' asked Hermux. 'I'd like to sit down for a minute.'

'Fine,' said Birch. 'You sit. I'll go and look for a log.'

Linka set down her buckets and stepped over in front of the small, plain door.

She asked, 'Did you try the doorknob, Birch? Maybe it's not locked.' She stooped over and grasped the handle. It turned easily in her paw.

She pushed, and the door swung open without a sound.

Chapter 61
BREAK TIME

An odd dry scent wafted from the dark interior. Hermux sniffed tentatively. It wasn't familiar, and it wasn't entirely pleasant.

Linka stooped slightly and peered inside. She started forward.

'Wait,' said Birch. 'We don't know what we're going to find. We'll need flashlights for sure.'

'You're right,' she said. 'And water, just in case.'

'And a snack for sure,' said Hermux.

'All right,' said Birch. 'Let's go back to camp. But let's hurry up. Five minutes to pack.'

Hermux wasted no time filling his canteen from the water can. Then he turned his mind to food, rifling quickly through the kitchen box. He filled a bag with raisins. He took a whole box of corn toast and a tin of dry-roasted mealy worms. Then he opened a jar of Stinky Cheese and ate a big spoonful on the spot.

'Mmmm,' he said. 'That is tasty! Maybe just one more.'

He ran to his tent and packed his backpack with a flashlight, a pocketknife, a compass and an extra handkerchief. He looked around for anything else that might be useful. His eye fell on the escape wheel. He picked it up and slipped it carefully into his pack.

'If this is an important clue, we may as well have it along with us,' he thought. Then he rushed back to the door, arriving there just behind Birch and Linka.

'All right,' said Birch, who had a large coil of rope slung over one shoulder. 'Let's go slowly, and everyone stay close together. Don't touch anything, if you can help it.'

He crouched down and squeezed through the door. Linka followed. Hermux brought up the rear.

After the bright sunlight it took a moment to adjust to the darkness inside. The beams of their flashlights nervously swept the floor, the walls and the ceiling.

They found themselves in a small entry hall.

'Imagine,' said Linka in a hushed voice. 'We are probably the first mice to set foot in here in more than three thousand years.'

An open doorway in the back wall led to a narrow staircase cut into the solid rock. Birch peered up the stairs.

'Can you see anything?' Hermux asked.

'Nope. Nothing but steps.' He started up, with Linka and Hermux following close behind. The stairs were very steep, and there was no handrail. They had hardly climbed twenty steps before Hermux began to wonder about the wisdom of carrying the extra weight of the escape wheel.

'How much higher do you think this goes?' he asked.

'It looks like we're about halfway up to a landing,' Birch told him. 'Yes. There's definitely a room up ahead.'

It turned out to be quite a large room, and it was furnished. There were three square wooden tables with little wooden chairs. One wall was lined with a row of benches. At the end of the benches stood a short cot topped by a thin mattress and a pillow.

'Look,' said Linka, shining her light on the pillow. 'You can still see the impression of someone's head.'

Hermux smacked the mattress with the flat of his hand, raising a cloud of dust. 'Whoever they were,' he coughed, 'they liked their mattresses hard.'

'Don't touch anything!' Birch warned again. 'You could destroy valuable historical material.'

'I'm sorry,' said Hermux. 'But somehow I was expecting more. This doesn't look like anything.'

Birch was examining the far wall.

'I think we've found the employee lounge,' he said. 'Listen to this: "Clean-up crew! It has come to the attention of the management that some of you have been dumping your sand inside the canyon. This will not be tolerated. Urns are to be emptied promptly on the hour. Sandboxes in the men's and women's lounges should be cleaned and changed twice daily. Have a nice day!"'

'The tone of that sounds so familiar,' said Linka. 'I wonder if Tucka is not the reincarnation of a prehistoric library manager.'

Next to the bulletin board stood a row of brooms made of rushes and twigs. By each broom was a bucket.

'There's a door over here,' said Linka.

Above the door was a handwritten sign.

'"Please remove your shoes before entering the library,"' Birch read carefully.

Hermux bent down to untie his shoes.

'I think we can break the rules this once,' said Linka. 'We don't work here.'

Chapter 62
GETTING THE PICTURE

They entered single file and stopped just inside the door, instinctively drawing closer to one another as they grasped the enormous scale of the empty space before them. The beams of their flashlights offered the merest pinpricks against an impenetrable sheet of darkness.

Finally Birch spoke. 'This must be it. We're in the library.'

'I can't see a thing,' said Hermux. The fur prickled on Hermux's neck and up and down his arms. It was exactly the kind of darkness that he didn't care for. 'It certainly seems large enough. And dark enough.'

'It's fantastic!' said Linka. 'It's huge! It must be eight storeys tall in here.' She pointed her light towards the ceiling. High above them faint glints of gold flickered back.

'It's painted!' said Hermux, adding his light to hers.

'It's a starry sky!' said Birch as the beam of his flashlight revealed a span of cobalt blue sparkling with brilliant gold stars.

'It's beautiful,' said Linka.

'Very beautiful,' agreed Hermux in an awestruck voice. The

stars seemed to group and regroup themselves in a shifting pattern of constellations.

Keeping their lights focused together, they brought them down the wall, backing their way slowly towards the centre of the room as band after band of images appeared.

Figures appeared. They seemed freshly painted, standing out in sharp relief against the flat background of a flowing river and an empty sky. They went about their daily lives as though their world had been cut into perfect ribbons, preserved and re-assembled into a brilliant striped quilt.

'Oh!' said Linka. She clutched Hermux's arm. 'Those are mice!'

And they were. Hundreds of them. In scene after scene, mice were harvesting grain, grinding wheat, baking bread, rowing boats and catching fish. They were gathering cattails and binding them into bunches. They were carrying wood and tending fires. They were hauling and digging. They were playing musical instruments. They were dancing.

'And those must be cats!' said Birch, pointing his light at one of the great furry and fanged creatures that presided over each scene. Solid, striped, spotted and calico. Tawny, black, white, grey and ginger. Long-haired, short-haired and nearly hairless. Cats were dining at banquet tables. They were lying in the sun. They were listening to music. They were curled up in reed baskets. They were being served and fed and combed and groomed by mice. They were being rowed in boats by mice. They were being carried on sedan chairs and pulled in chariots. They were giving orders to mice. And guarding mice. And punishing them with clubs and whips.

'This doesn't look very nice at all,' said Hermux. He stared forlornly at a mouse about his own age whose collar was chained to a grindstone. Hermux pulled uncomfortably at the neck of his shirt. 'We look like slaves.'

'We don't just look like slaves,' Linka said grimly. 'We were slaves.'

Chapter 63
OFF THE SHELF

'I don't know if I want to find a king's mummy,' Linka said. 'After seeing this, I certainly don't want to bring one back to life.'

'I'm not so interested in finding a dead king. We can leave him for Tucka and Hinkum,' said Birch. 'But I would like to find his library. That does interest me. And if we're going to stake first claim on it, we'd better get to it. I suggest we stay near to the wall and make a circuit of the room ... if it is a room. That should give us an idea of the layout. Then we can go from there. For the time being, I think it's better to stay close together. I'll take the lead. Linka, you keep your light on the wall. Hermux, you keep your light on the interior, and everyone count your steps as we go so we can get an idea of size and distance.'

They assumed a wedge formation and began to move forward, cautiously following the wall.

'There's something out in the room,' said Hermux. 'It's big, but it doesn't seem to be moving.' His flashlight picked out the faint lines of a structure. 'It looks like a house. Or the frame of a house.'

Their lights converged on a maze of columns that rose from

the floor. The vague shapes of a large roof and several small ones hung suspended in the shadows above.

'It's not a house,' said Linka, craning her neck for a better view. 'It's a table. A gigantic library table. And chairs.'

'Of course,' said Birch.

'Right,' said Hermux with a shiver. 'A library table. A big one. I should have guessed. Then that must be the librarian's desk coming up.' He pointed towards a massive block of stone that loomed ahead. It resembled a small office building with cat-tail columns set at each corner. Carved into its face was the silhouette of a seated cat. Over its head floated a crown. It was framed by vertical rows of symbols.

'"I, King Ka-Narsh-Pah,"' Birch read solemnly, '"Eye-of-Heaven, Talon-of-Justice, Strength-of-Many, Merciful-Paw and Father-of-All, in the twentieth year of my reign, built this library to celebrate the accomplishments of my people and preserve for eternity the glory of our science, literature, history and art."' Birch took a deep breath and sobbed with a mix of relief and regret.

'I wish Mirrin could be here to see this,' said Hermux, patting him kindly on the shoulder. 'She would be so proud of you!'

'Yes,' said Birch. 'I think she would be. I've dreamed about this moment for almost my whole life. And now that it's here, it still feels like I'm dreaming.'

They continued their exploration of the room. It was an extended rectangle with adjoining rooms on each end. The long walls were broken by a broad stairway on one side and a matching hallway on the other that led back into the mountain. They eventually found themselves back at the small door to the employee lounge.

'Where are the books?' asked Hermux.

'Scrolls, not books,' said Birch. 'And my guess is that they're stored in the end rooms. I think this was the main reading room. It's time to look in the stacks.'

They began with the room nearest to them.

'Look at the mural above the door,' Birch told them. 'A cat studying the heavens and making notes. And the symbol beside it. The eye and the scale. I believe that must be *science*.'

'All right!' said Hermux. 'To the greatest discovery in history! And the greatest discoverer!' He bowed slightly towards Birch, and gestured for Birch to enter first.

Birch's hand trembled so badly that Linka was afraid he would drop his flashlight. She took it from him and said, 'Here, why don't I hold your light so you have both hands free.'

Inside the room they found four rows of shelves that rose to the ceiling. A tremendously tall ladder leaned against the first.

'All right,' said Birch hopefully. 'Here goes.'

Grasping the one side of the ladder, he began to climb. When he reached the height of the first shelf, he leaned over.

'Hand me a light,' he said soberly.

Hermux climbed up behind him and passed him his flashlight. Birch swept the light over the length of the shelf. Then, without saying a word, he climbed up to the next one.

'What do you see?' cried Linka impatiently.

'Nothing,' said Birch in a broken voice.

'What do you mean, nothing?' demanded Hermux.

'There's nothing here. The shelves are completely empty!'

Chapter 64
IN A PINCH

'Maybe they're all checked out?' Hermux suggested.

'Maybe I should never have been born!' wailed Birch, and buried his face in his paws.

'Don't give up yet!' said Linka. 'There's still the other room to search, and the hallway. The books here could have been moved. Or maybe this section was never even used. Hermux, you run down and check the room at the other end. Birch, you just rest here with me for a moment. Then we'll meet Hermux in the middle at the entrance to the hall. Hermux can give us a report. And then we'll all stop and sit down and have something to eat. We're all tired from the digging and the excitement.'

She helped Birch down from the ladder and motioned for Hermux to be on his way. Hermux hesitated.

'You mean by myself, don't you?' asked Hermux.

Linka nodded.

'OK,' he said. 'I mean, what is there to be afraid of? The place has been empty for thousands of years. It's just a big dark room. Right? Right! All right! I'll be going. And we'll all meet in the middle. Soon!'

He started off boldly into the darkness, shining his flashlight from side to side on the floor ahead. But by the time he had reached the first library table, his boldness was beginning to fade. Alone, the room felt even bigger and darker. One light against the darkness was not nearly as reassuring as three. And it was not as silent as he remembered it. Maybe it was Linka and Birch talking in the distance. Maybe it was the echo of his footsteps. Maybe it was just his own heavy breathing. But there was something restless in the air. Some faint feathery noise that he couldn't quite put his finger on.

He slowed down, and the noise faded away. He speeded up, and it seemed to return.

He stopped cold and arched his ears. He turned in a slow circle with his flashlight focused in the distance. There! Something pale appeared to float by and vanish. He strained his eyes to see. There it was again. The light wavered. There was nothing there.

'I'm imagining things,' he told himself. 'It's the darkness. Like Mirrin said, it's not empty. Especially when you're alone.'

He shook his head and scooted along. He passed the stairs and reached the corner of the room. He turned and followed the wall to the doorway.

The mural above the door depicted a cat standing at an easel and observing a sunset. Next to it were an eye and a paintbrush.

'Art,' he thought. 'Mirrin would like that. Maybe the cats were long on art and short on science.'

But they were not. A short look around in the art stacks showed the shelves to be utterly bare.

'Oh!' he said miserably. 'I don't want to be the one to break the news to Birch.'

He trudged slowly back towards the centre of the room. Two small lights were visible as he approached.

211

'Hermux?' called Linka. 'What did you find?'

Birch waited for Hermux to speak.

'Birch,' Hermux began uncomfortably.

'Never mind, Hermux. I know what you're going to say. Sit down and have something to eat.'

Hermux dropped his backpack on the floor.

'It's still an amazing discovery,' said Hermux. He popped a handful of raisins in his mouth and opened the tin of mealy worms, which he offered to Birch.

'Hermux is right,' Linka added. 'You proved your point. There was a civilization of cats. Although it looks like it was only civilized as far as the cats went.'

'I know,' said Birch forlornly. He passed the worms to Linka. 'But I had my heart set on the scrolls. I can't stay out here the rest of my life. I was planning on taking the scrolls back to Pinchester and settling down to work on the translations.'

'I know that would make Mirrin happy,' said Hermux, getting to his feet. 'Have you searched this hall yet? It looks like there are two more rooms. And look. There's a portrait of the king on the back wall. With a big urn on each side.'

Hermux started towards one of the urns.

'It just occurred to me,' he said, turning back. 'You don't think they cremated him, do you? Tucka won't like that!'

Hermux felt it before he saw it. And what he saw was only a yellow blur. Something large scuttling towards him from the doorway on the right. It hit him hard, knocking the flashlight from his paw. It seized him by the neck and slammed him against the wall.

He barely had enough breath to cry out.

'Hermux!' said Linka. 'What happened?'

She and Birch grabbed their flashlights and leapt to their feet.

What they saw astonished them. A horrifying crablike creature with six scrabbling legs, a flat segmented body, an arching tail and two monstrous claws. One of them was clamped viciously around Hermux's neck. The other waved threateningly in the air. Two small, evil eyes protruded from its tiny head.

'Birch! What on earth is it?' Linka screamed.

'It's a scorpion!' said Birch. 'Watch out for the tail! It's poisonous!' He grabbed his rope. Then, tying it into a loop, he inched his way closer to the creature. He swung the rope in a wide arc and lassoed the scorpion's tail.

'I've got it,' he yelled. But he spoke too soon. With an insolent flick the scorpion whipped its tail. Birch flew through the air and landed on his head.

'Birch!' shouted Linka.

He lay motionless on the floor.

'Linka!' Hermux gurgled. 'Shoot it!'

'We don't have a gun!'

'Stab it!'

'I don't have a knife!'

'There's a knife in my pack!'

Linka dug furiously through Hermux's pack. She found the knife and opened it. It was a cheese knife. She gritted her teeth in pure frustration.

Her hand touched the cool metal of the bronze escape wheel. She felt the sharp points of its teeth. She grabbed it firmly in hand and stood. The scorpion eyed her coldly. Its free pincer opened and closed with a sharp click. Then it turned back to Hermux. Its tail flicked in warning. A single drop of venom glistened at its tip.

Linka took a deep breath. Then she twisted suddenly. She dropped back on one leg and launched herself forward, unwinding from the waist. She released the gear with a hard snap of her wrist.

It sailed through the air like a buzz saw, severing the scorpion's pincer and slicing off its head before it smashed into one of the urns. The urn broke into pieces and spilled sand all over the floor.

Hermux wrested the pincer from his neck and staggered free.

He gasped for air.

'Thank you!' he wheezed. 'That was brilliant!'

One by one the scorpion's legs collapsed. Its lifeless body sagged to the floor. But its tail still arched in the air.

'Now I think I'm going to be sick,' said Hermux.

Finally, the scorpion's tail collapsed. It fell with a violent twitch, landing heavily against the frame of the king's portrait and knocking it crooked.

There was a peculiar whirring sound of machinery, followed by a dull clunk. Then the king's portrait began to slide to one side. It vanished into the wall, revealing a doorway. Beyond it a wide set of stone stairs rose and vanished into darkness.

Chapter 65
GOING UP!

Woozy as he was, Birch would not hear of returning to camp until they discovered where the stairs led.

'Tucka and Hinkum may arrive at any minute,' he complained as Linka gently examined the knot on his head. 'Besides, it's not the first time I've been knocked out. I've come this far. I'm going up there if I have to crawl on my hands and knees. Watch out for that stinger, Hermux. It can still be lethal.'

Hermux flinched. He had tied Birch's rope around the scorpion's body and was attempting to pull it clear of the opening in the wall.

'I can't budge it,' he said finally. 'Maybe if all three of us try ...'

'I can help,' insisted Birch. He tried to stand.

'You just sit there a minute,' Linka insisted. 'And let me bind this with a wet handkerchief. It will help reduce the swelling.'

Hermux had an idea. The spilled sand from the broken urn had made the floor around it slippery. Hermux filled both hands with sand and sprinkled it generously in the path of the scorpion.

'This might give us a little lubrication,' he explained as they formed themselves into a tow chain.

'OK! On the count of three!'

Pitting their combined bodies against the dead weight of the scorpion's remains, they threw themselves against the rope. The unwieldy corpse dislodged with a jerk and slid towards them. They dragged it, one tug at a time, out of the hall and into the main reading room.

Hermux stepped over the remaining claw and untied Birch's rope. He coiled it and returned it to Birch.

'Normally, after this much work, I'd want a snack. But,' he said, eyeing the scorpion's outstretched tail with its needle-like stinger, 'I seem to have lost my appetite. For now, anyway. By the way, why do you think they kept sand in the urns? There's plenty outside.'

'They had some kind of fixation with fresh sand,' said Linka. 'Remember the notice in the lounge. The urns are to be emptied regularly and the sandboxes changed. Look, there are even spouts above the urns for refilling them.'

'That's odd,' said Hermux. 'That means they must store sand somewhere above here.'

They turned their attention to the stairs.

'Well, these are much too big for us,' Birch said. 'I can't even reach the top of one.'

'But here are the service stairs,' said Hermux, shining his light at a mouse-sized set of steps cut into a gutter at the side of the main stairs. 'Next stop, second floor! Housewares and tomb supplies!'

However, the next stop turned out to be much further than the second floor. By the time they reached the top of the stairs, it seemed that they had climbed more than ten floors at the very least.

'I'm afraid I've got to sit a minute,' admitted Birch.

'Good,' said Linka. 'I can't go another inch.'

'Me neither,' said Hermux, easing himself to the floor. 'But I think I've got my appetite back. Would anyone like a corn toast?'

'Sounds yummy,' said Linka. 'So, Birch, where are we?'

'I think we're in the private quarters of the king. That explains the secret entrance.'

'You mean his private quarters while he was alive? Or after?' asked Hermux. 'I mean, what exactly does a dead king do in a tomb, anyway?'

'I guess we're about to find out ...'

Chapter 66
THE KING'S DELIGHT

They found themselves in a series of rooms that led away from the stairs. They explored them cautiously one by one. The rooms were small compared to the library below. The walls were painted in brilliant colours. But the paintings here were softer and less stylized. A single scene continued from wall to wall around each room. The first room was a landscape of fields, orchards and vineyards with the river flowing smoothly behind it all.

The next room was a city with broad streets and trees and great buildings and temples supported by reed columns.

The third room was a palace surrounded by a high wall. It had gardens and fountains and towers and gilded pavilions.

The fourth room was larger. It was a theatre. But it had only one seat. An enormous throne stood on a raised platform against one wall. On the throne sat a gigantic, gleaming, golden cat.

Its jewelled eyes stared straight ahead at a small stage with a tattered curtain.

'Ka-Narsh-Pah!' said Birch.

'The king's mummy!' said Hermux. He approached it with extreme caution. He stared up at it, watching for any signs of movement or life. 'It must have been incredibly powerful,' he said finally. 'I don't think I've ever felt so small.'

'What do you think is behind the curtain?' asked Linka from the front of the stage. She lifted the bottom to peek under and let loose a shriek that shook the walls of the tomb.

'Eeeek!' she screamed. 'It's a mouse!' She pointed at the curtain and screamed again. 'There's a mouse in there!'

Hermux ran to her side and pulled at the curtain. It tore from its supports and dropped to the floor in a choking cloud of rotten dust.

Standing in the centre of the stage, staring back at the king, stood a beautiful young mouse. She wore golden slippers on her tiny feet, a heavy necklace of turquoise beads and a spangled halter. One arm was raised above her head in a carefree salute, and on her curious, lifelike face was painted a mysterious and sad smile.

Chapter 67
HEAD OVER HEELS

'Of course, I knew she wasn't real,' Linka insisted with a nervous laugh. 'I was just so surprised. It was the last thing I expected to see. And you have to admit that at first glance she looks very convincing.'

Hermux didn't argue. His heart was still pounding madly. For one single instant, no matter how short it was, he had been convinced that she was a real, living, breathing mouse who had miraculously survived three thousand years in a sealed tomb and rejoiced in her deliverance. The shock faded. But the wonder of it did not.

She was without a doubt the most lifelike mechanism he had ever seen. She appeared to be a dancer suspended in the middle of a leaping turn. One leg reached out for the floor. The other extended back and up. Her arms seemed to float effortlessly in the air. One rose above her head. The other was flung out to the side. She tilted her head slightly and gazed calmly at her captive audience of one. In a sinuous line around her, spiralled her long, graceful tail.

Hermux was saddened to see that her right eye was missing. The glass or stone had fallen from its golden socket.

'Hermux,' said Linka, 'have you heard a single word we've said?'

'Of course,' he answered. 'Watch your step walking around. She's missing one eye. It's probably on the floor somewhere.'

'Then who do you think should stay here and stand guard while the others go back to camp? Birch needs his camera equipment to document this. I want to check on Tucka and Hinkum's progress. Just in case. We can't let them barge in here and take over.'

'I'll stay here,' said Hermux dreamily. 'Restore the "King's Delight". That's what this is, isn't it? The King's Delight! A dancing mouse. Why would he choose a mouse? Mice were slaves. Why not a dancing cat?'

'You won't be nervous alone here with the mummy?' Birch asked.

Hermux had forgotten all about the mummy.

No. He shook his head.

'We may not be back for hours,' warned Birch.

'I'll be OK,' said Hermux. 'Did you notice how they made her fingers jointed on each paw?'

'There's not a lot left to eat,' Linka told him.

'I'm not hungry. Did you get a good look at the tail? There must be a thousand sections hinged together.'

'You may get hungry.'

'No. I won't. Just leave some water. I wonder what drives it? There's got to be a power source. Didn't you say you saw a reservoir or something up on top?'

'Yes. It looked like a cistern. Are you sure you're all right?' Linka asked. 'You're not having some kind of stress reaction, are you? From the scorpion fight?'

'No. No. I'm fine. What kind of tools do you have in the

plane? What size wrenches? Of course, I don't even know if they would have used bolts. What did you do with the escape wheel?'

'Hermux! Pay attention! I'm leaving you my canteen. It's right here! Now, if we're not back in three hours, you come out! And if Tucka and Hinkum manage to get in here through some other entrance, you stand your ground.'

'That's right, Hermux,' Birch added. 'I don't care if they are starting their own museum. We are now official representatives of the Perriflot Institute, which is undertaking this expedition on behalf of the Pinchester Museum. If they have problems, they can take it up with Ortolina Perriflot herself. And Mirrin tells me she is a force to be reckoned with. Even for Hinkum and Tucka.'

Hermux nodded pleasantly. 'Right,' he said. 'I'll stand my ground. What kind of tools do you think they had? How did they get the fur to look so real? Did you see the tracks on the floor? It looks like she can dance the width of the entire stage. Can you imagine that? Dancing here in the dark for all eternity?'

Birch and Linka had donned their packs and were preparing to depart when the sound of heavy footsteps sounded in the outer rooms.

'Oh, no!' said Linka. 'They're here! All right, everyone. Stand firm!' Her eyes flashed with determination.

A mouse stepped through the doorway. He wore a metal tank on his back. His face was obscured by a gas mask.

'It's all right, Hinkum,' said Birch. 'The air is perfectly breathable. We haven't had any problems. But as you can see, we got here first. Fair and square. And we don't intend to leave!'

222

'It won't be necessary,' said the mouse, removing his gas mask.

'Hey! You're not Hinkum!' said Hermux. 'You're the mouse supremacist! How did you get here?'

'I could ask you the same thing.'

'Well, what do you want?'

'Just doing a little pest control!' he snickered. 'I told you I'd get even!' He pulled the gas mask back down over his face and released a knob on the tank.

There was a loud hiss, and Hermux smelled something sweet and heavy billowing into the air. It reminded him of fresh sheets and clean pyjamas. It was a nice, drowsy smell. Hermux's eyes suddenly felt very heavy. Then he decided to lie down. It had been a long, long day. And he was very tired.

The last thing he remembered was reading the lettering on the side of the mouse's tank.

Night-Night!

Safe, fast and effective

From the experts in crowd control

Chapter 68
EXPLOSIVE SITUATION

'Hermux?'

'Hmmmn?'

'Can you hear me?'

'What?'

'Wake up!'

Hermux opened his eyes.

'Goodness! I must have dozed off!' he said with a yawn. 'Excuse me.'

'You didn't doze off,' Linka said. 'We were knocked out.'

'Oh. Now I remember. It was that mouse from the Brotherhood of Mice. The one that started all the trouble at the museum.'

'I don't know who it was. But I don't like him. Can you move?'

'Oh my gosh! I'm paralysed! I can't move my arms! Or my legs! What did he do to us?'

'He tied us up.'

'Oh. You're right. Where's Birch?'

'I can't see him.'

'Birch?'

'Birch? Where are you?'

'I'm right here behind these boxes. I've got a headache. A miserable headache.'

'Can you see anything? Is there anyone here?'

'I don't see anybody. It looks like there's a lantern in the next room.'

'What are all these boxes, anyway?' asked Linka.

'This one's got printing on it,' said Hermux. 'It says "Dancer". Do you think he's going to steal the dancing mouse?'

'This one next to me says "Keep away from ..." But I can't see what. Your feet are in the way, Hermux.'

'Let me see if I can scooch up here.'

'That's better. It says, "Keep away from flames."'

'But the dancer is not flammable. She's all metal,' said Hermux. 'Probably gold.'

'I'm afraid it's not the dancer,' said Birch wearily. 'I can read the whole box now.'

'What does it say?' asked Hermux.

'It says "Danger! Keep away from flames. DYNAMITE."'

'Oh,' said Linka.

'That's not good, is it?' said Hermux. 'The Brotherhood of Mice is going to blow up the tomb! But how did they follow us here?'

'Maybe they didn't follow us, Hermux. They have the scroll and all my notes from the hotel.'

'We've got to get out here!' said Linka. 'I've got –'

'Sssshhh!' said Hermux. 'Someone's coming. Be careful what you say! They must be insane!'

Heavy footsteps approached and then a brilliant light filled the doorway.

'What have we here?' someone asked. 'Tentintrotter? Is that

225

you?' He put the lantern down. 'And Tantamoq, isn't it? The watchmaker? What on earth brings you to these parts?'

It was Hinkum Stepfitchler. He was immaculately dressed in a pressed khaki safari jacket, long shorts and high-laced boots.

'Oh! Thank goodness!' Hermux exclaimed.

'You've come just in time!' said Birch.

Hinkum approached the mummy of Ka-Narsh-Pah. 'Well, well, well,' he mused. 'I certainly didn't expect to actually find this. Congratulations! How in the world did you find the entrance to the tomb?'

'Never mind that!' snapped Birch. 'Get us untied before they get back.'

'Before who gets back?' asked Hinkum.

'The mouse supremacists!' Hermux explained. 'The Brotherhood of Mice. One of them gassed us and tied us up. He's the one who started the riot at the museum. They broke into Birch's hotel room and stole the scroll and Birch's notebooks. They're mad. They hate cats. They're going to blow the place up! Just for spite! And us with it! To get even with us for having one of them arrested. Hurry and get us loose!'

'Now, let's not be hasty,' Hinkum began, sitting down on one of the boxes. 'I hate to interfere with someone else's work. You say someone is planning an explosion of some sort?'

'Be careful!' pleaded Hermux. 'This may be dynamite.'

'Oh, it most certainly is dynamite,' Hinkum said cheerfully. 'It says so right here on the box.'

'Then untie us before something terrible happens!'

'It might not be so terrible.'

'Of course it would be terrible! This whole place would be destroyed and we would all be killed!' said Linka.

226

'You have to admit it's an unusual idea. Just to blow it all up. Think of it! Nobody would ever know it had existed.'

'Obviously you've got to stop it!' argued Linka.

'I don't believe we've been introduced,' said Stepfitchler with a slight bow. 'I'm Hinkum Stepfitchler the Third. And you are?'

'Linka Perflinger.'

'Ms Perflinger is a well-known adventuress, daredevil and aviatrix,' Hermux added proudly.

'Well, Ms Perflinger, I'd say you're having yourself quite an adventure this time,' Hinkum replied.

'And I'd like to get out of it alive. If you don't mind.'

'Ah! But I'm afraid I do mind,' said Hinkum mildly. 'There is the question of what to do with all of this.' He stopped a moment and regarded the gold mummy and the dancing mouse on her threadbare stage. He shrugged.

'All right!' Birch conceded. 'Take it all! It's yours! Put it in your stupid museum! You and Tucka win! At least I'll have the satisfaction of knowing I was right. And the world will know too!'

'But that is precisely what must never happen!' said Hinkum. He leaned back on one of the dynamite crates and lit a cigarette.

'Put that out!' said Hermux. 'You could blow us all to king-dom come!'

'Eventually I will, Mr Tantamoq. You can count on it. In the meantime, don't worry yourself. I grew up with dynamite. You seem to forget that my great-great-aunt Hissy invented it. This is some of the last of her own private stock. First-rate stuff too! It should make quite the big bang.'

Chapter 69
TRUE CONFESSIONS

Hinkum looked at his watch.

'I've really got to hurry. Tucka is expecting me back for an intimate little dinner before the ceremony. And I've got to change into formal wear. Did I tell you? Today's my wedding day!'

'Congratulations,' said Hermux sourly.

'You're all invited, of course! But I can see that you're tied up for the evening. Or should I say "indefinitely"?'

'Why are you doing this?' demanded Linka.

'Now that is a good question. I'll have to think about it for a moment.' Hinkum stubbed out his cigarette on the dynamite box. 'But just let me get this fuse set first. I always have to concentrate on this part. Mistakes can be so messy.'

Hinkum pried open one of the boxes and removed a stick of dynamite.

'You're a cad to do this, Stepfitchler!' Hermux said.

'No, Mr Tantamoq. I'm a Stepfitchler. It's altogether different. I'm just doing what should have been done eight hundred years ago. Of course, we hadn't invented dynamite then. So now it falls to me to get it done. Everyone expects Hinkum to clean up their messes. Now, back to Ms Perflinger's question. Why am I doing this? Can anyone guess?'

'Because you're a lunatic?' Birch asked.

'Calling names, Tentintrotter? Shame on you. I expected more! Perhaps you're not quite as bright as Father thought!'

'Your father thought I was bright?' Birch sounded amazed.

'The most brilliant student of his entire career!' Hinkum said sarcastically. 'A truly gifted scholar. The son he'd always wanted to carry on his work. Even though you're a chipmunk. That was hard for him at first, but he got over it. What he never quite got over was having to destroy you! Poor, poor Father! But it's a long story. I really should start at the beginning. After all, I'm only going to tell it once. You'll be the only people outside the family that will ever hear it. And when you're gone, which shouldn't be long now, it will be lost and forgotten forever.

'It all began right here more than eight hundred years ago. Roto Stepfitchler, my illustrious ancestor, was a shepherd living in a village somewhere downriver from here. It was a poor village, and the Stepfitchlers were among the poorest. Roto had a small herd of grasshoppers. Have you ever eaten grasshopper meat, Ms Perflinger?'

'On occasion,' she said. She had once survived for a week on wild grasshopper. She had shot it and butchered it herself.

'I've never cared for it,' said Hinkum. 'Too tough and gamy. Grasshoppers are stupid, wilful animals. Although they'll eat anything that's green. But back to the story. One spring, Roto got the bright idea of moving his herd to the top of the canyon to graze them there. No one had ever done it. Everyone warned him against it. They were right. The herd was scattered in a storm. Several of the grasshoppers took refuge in the canyon here. Roto tracked them. That's how he discovered the staircase

229

down the side and found the library. The rest is history. Literally in this case.

'Roto never said a word about what he had found. He returned to the village with a tale of woe – barren dunes and sandstorms and a lost herd. After that, no one would even set foot on the top of the canyon. From then on, Roto would slip away whenever he could to explore the library. He was fascinated by the engineering scrolls. He couldn't translate the script, but he could understand the drawings. The first thing he did was invent the wheel.'

'Don't you mean "reinvent the wheel"?' asked Hermux.

'I suppose so. If you want to be petty! In any case, after the wheel came the shovel and the rake, et cetera, et cetera, et cetera. It wasn't long before the Stepfitchlers were no longer poor. In fact, we were rich. And we've only got richer and richer ever since. At least until recently.'

'But what happened to the scrolls?' asked Birch. 'We didn't find any.'

'I'll get to that in a moment. In the meantime, the inventions were beginning to change things. They don't call us the Godfathers of Civilization for nothing. Then Roto's son, Rookum, invented the sundial and the compass, and he discovered the laws of geometry. That really got things moving. Cities began to grow, and Rookum wanted to be nearer the action. When Roto died, Rookum moved the family south. Before he left, he tunnelled through the wall at the end of the canyon, emptied every scrap of parchment from the library, loaded it on to a boat and took it all with him. You didn't know about the tunnel, did you, Tentintrotter? You had to use an aeroplane. Unfortunately, aeroplanes don't leave trails. It will be years and years before anyone ever finds your plane. If they ever do. But I'm getting ahead of my story. Eventually Rookum moved east and settled in Pinchester. As soon as he got there, he began building Stepfitchler Mansion, the greatest house in all the land. Beneath it he dug a secret basement. The scrolls have been there ever since.'

'You can't kill us just to keep the family secret!' said Linka.

'That's where you're wrong. I certainly can. And I will. It's not just a family secret. It's our shared sense of history. It's not just mine. It's yours too. Who invented the printing press?'

'Hinkum Stepfitchler the First,' Hermux recited dutifully.

'Who discovered gravity?'

'Sir Boosik Stepfitchler,' admitted Linka.

'Who invented the clock, the microscope, the telescope and the gyroscope?'

'Hinkum Stepfitchler the Second,' said Birch ruefully.

'Who invented the steamboat?'

'Boomboom Stepfitchler.'

'And you want all of that destroyed? It would be too painful for everyone. They admire us. They envy us. We inspire them! You can't take that away!'

'But it's all a lie!' blurted Linka. 'You didn't invent any of it!'

'Well, actually, Aunt Hissy did invent dynamite. Although she claims it was a baking accident. So you're wrong there. And besides, that misses the point. Do you want schoolchildren being taught that mice didn't invent the world? That some strange creature in the past made most of the great discoveries? What earthly good would that do?'

'If that is the truth, then why not?' demanded Hermux.

'You ask that even after you've seen how cats treated mice?'

That was a hard question.

'Don't our lives count for anything?' asked Birch.

231

'I'd say your life has counted altogether too much!' Hinkum turned to Birch. 'This is entirely your fault, you know. Things were going very nicely until you came along. We had exhausted all the scientific possibilities of the scrolls. But we still had some money coming in from Aunt Hissy's dynamite. Father was set up at the university. And he was beginning to make some real progress in translating the Cat language. Then you show up. The most gifted linguist Father had ever encountered. And he was supposed to be the big genius. "Why can't you be more like Birch?" he would ask me. "Look how hard he works. Look at the way he studies every night." So I did. I watched you. I studied you. And one night when you dozed off, I slipped into the library and left the little map for you to find. The map that Father had been poring over for more than a year, struggling to translate a single line. Then you translate it in less than a month! That was your first big mistake. You injured his pride. And Father was a very proud mouse. He would eventually have forgiven you. But you had to be the big showoff! That was your second mistake. You had to be right! Everyone had to know how smart Birch Tentintrotter was! The first chipmunk professor of Old Mouse! It turned out that you were just a little too smart for your own good!

'Still, after all that, Father went before the family and made a case for you. He even said that the time might have finally come to tell the true story of the Stepfitchlers and their library. That you might be able to finally unlock the mystery of the Cat hieroglyphs. He argued that the library was a national treasure. A cultural treasure that belonged to the world. Perhaps it was time to share it. Fortunately for all of us, Stepfitchler family decisions were made democratically. We took a vote. It was the first time I got to vote at a family meeting. It was very close.

Father could be very persuasive when he wanted to be. I got to cast the deciding vote. So I did. You had to be destroyed. It was a question of family values. I don't think Father ever quite recovered from reading about your little boating accident. It's a pity you didn't just stay dead when you had the chance.'

Chapter 70
WEDDING PLANS

'You're bluffing!' said Linka. 'I saw you unloading the crate from the boat. You're here for the statue. We know you promised it to Tucka.'

'How perceptive of you. But I haven't forgotten Tucka. How could I? She is expecting a big surprise in that crate. And believe me, she'll get one. Struff is preparing it now. Struff is not really a mouse supremacist, you know. He's actually a very modest mouse. Just a working guy with bills to pay. But I think he's been very convincing so far. Don't you?'

'What kind of surprise for Tucka?' asked Hermux suspiciously.

'Well, suppose that something unfortunate were to happen to Tucka once we're married. What do you suppose would happen to all her money and her cosmetics empire?'

'As her husband, you would inherit it,' said Linka disdainfully.

'Exactly!' said Hinkum. 'And believe me, although I wouldn't admit this to another soul in the world, I could really use the money.'

'But you're the sole heir of the Stepfitchler fortune!' said Hermux incredulously. 'Why do you need more money?'

'It's not cheap being a Stepfitchler. There's a lot of upkeep. We've sunk a fortune into that ridiculous university. And our last patent – Aunt Hissy's dynamite – ran out this year. It's fitting, don't you think, that I'm using her dynamite to get a fresh start.'

'But you didn't say what Tucka's surprise will be,' Hermux reminded him.

'Her surprise? Tonight, after all the excitement of the wedding celebration, someone on the SS *Beauty Queen* is going to get careless. It happens all the time on riverboats. Doesn't it, Birch? I'm afraid it's going to spring a leak and go down with all hands on board. Everyone will be much too sleepy to swim. Tucka will be spending her eternity at the bottom of the Longish River, nailed into a crate of rocks. I'll manage to swim to shore, of course, clutching all that remains of my dear departed wife – our marriage certificate.

'For a while I'll be grief-stricken. I'll retire into seclusion at the mansion in Pinchester. I'll spend my days staring moodily into the fireplace until I've burnt every single last scrap of Cat scroll. And then it will be done. The Stepfitchler legacy will be safe forever. And that's the end of my little story. Now it's time for the end of yours. Don't worry about a wedding present. I totally understand.'

Hinkum unrolled the fuse across the floor and out of the door. Then he came back. He crawled up on to the stage and eyed the dancing mouse. Then he grabbed her head with both hands and wrenched it off.

'Stop!' growled Hermux. 'Don't hurt her! She's a masterpiece!'

'And I'll bet the museum will pay a pretty penny for her,' Hinkum said. 'At least enough to tide me over until Tucka's estate is settled. I'll make up a nice little story about a portrait head of my great-great-great-great-grandmother. It looks like gold too.'

'Put that back!' said Birch. 'It's priceless. It's part of history.'

'It's part of mouse history,' Hinkum snarled. 'What difference does it make to you? You're not even a mouse!'

'It's part of my history too,' Birch said indignantly. 'We're all one people.'

'That's right!' said Hinkum. 'You are all one people – the losers! Just like the cats! So this little bit of loser history disappears. Who will care? Who will even know?'

'We will!' said Hermux.

'I'm afraid you're wrong. In a few minutes you will neither know nor care. Now, night-night and sweet dreams,' he called over his shoulder. 'Incidentally, anybody got a match? Ha! Ha! Ha!'

His footsteps receded into the distance. They heard the low rumble of the stone door of the tomb sliding back into place. And then the sound of hammering.

'He's wedging the door shut,' Linka said hopelessly.

Chapter 71
A FAMILIAR RING

'We're trapped,' said Linka.

'There's no way out,' Hermux agreed.

'No chance of escape.'

'We're doomed.'

'It's hopeless.'

'This is goodbye, kid,' said Hermux with an effort to sound brave.

'It was a good adventure, Hermux.'

'It really was!'

'I've enjoyed every bit of it.'

'Really? Me too.'

'I enjoyed spending time with you.'

'The best part was getting to know you better.'

'I feel the same,' sighed Linka. 'Gee, it seems like only yesterday that we were tied up together for the first time.'

'It does, doesn't it,' said Hermux rather dreamily. 'But it was six months ago, wasn't it?'

'It was,' said Linka sweetly. She laughed. 'Seems like a lifetime, doesn't it?'

'Listen,' interrupted Birch, sniffing the air. 'I don't want to break up this intimate little chat, but it will be the end of all of our lifetimes if we don't do something, and fast!'

'Oh!' said Hermux. 'Right. Any ideas? I can hardly move. My hands are tied and my feet are tied and then my hands and feet are tied together. I'm glad you brought plenty of rope, Birch. They didn't have to skimp.'

'See if you can work your way closer to me,' Linka told him. 'Can you move your hands?'

'No. Not really,' she said. 'But I've got my ring on.'

'Your ring?'

'Remember? The ring you liked? I designed it and had it made as soon as I got out of the hospital after the Last Resort. Being a prisoner like that taught me a lesson. I told myself that if I ever got out of there, I would never be stupid enough to get caught again without some kind of backup. OK, can you move your fingers at all?'

'Yes. Barely.'

'Can you feel my ring?'

'Yes.'

'Get hold of the top of it and snap it open.'

'Like that?'

'That's it,' she said excitedly.

'Ouch! It's sharp.'

'It's supposed to be,' she explained. 'Six tiny carbide grit blades mounted side by side. They'd cut through steel cable if we had time. They ought to take care of these ropes.'

'Folks!' said Birch. 'I don't want to seem pushy, but the burning fuse has rounded the corner and is heading for us. If you're going to cut the rope, get on with it.'

'All right,' Linka told Hermux. 'I'll hold my hands steady.

You move your rope against the ring. It will cut better if you can keep the rope taut.'

Hermux extended his feet and held the rope as tight as a fiddle string. He sawed back and forth with his whole body.

'The fuse is four metres and approaching quickly,' Birch cautioned.

'Is it working?' asked Linka.

'I think so,' said Hermux. 'Just a little bit more.'

'Three metres and counting.'

'There!' said Hermux. 'That's it.'

'Two and a half!'

Hermux struggled to his feet. He hopped towards the fuse, tripped against the first case of dynamite and fell flat on his face.

'Hermux!' screamed Linka. 'Get up!'

'One metre!'

Hermux wormed his way forward on his stomach. Inches away from his face, the fuse snapped and sparked. He lunged ahead of the burning section and grabbed the fuse with his teeth. He lifted his head and gave a mighty yank. The fuse came loose with a snap, but it continued to burn, singing all the whiskers off the right side of Hermux's face and scorching his lips and tongue. He spat wildly. The fuse sputtered uselessly on the floor and died.

'Oww!' moaned Hermux. 'I burned my tongue.'

Chapter 72
DRIVING FORCE

Hermux helped Linka to her feet.

'I hate being tied up,' she said angrily. 'It's so humiliating. Oh, look at your lip! It's blistered. Does it hurt?'

'Not as much as my tongue,' said Hermux with a grimace.

Birch cleared his throat.

'I'm getting a little stiff here,' he said.

'Sorry,' said Hermux. 'I'll be right there.'

Once they were all free, they had to face the larger problem of how to escape from the tomb.

Hoping against hope, Hermux volunteered to return to the secret entrance and see if Hinkum had blocked the door.

'You two rest up and think,' he told them. He took a swig of water from his canteen. There was not much left. 'We need all our wits about us.'

Twenty minutes later he returned with bad news.

'It's no good. Hinkum hammered something into the door to wedge it shut. He was in such a hurry to get out that he left one of his lanterns behind. At least it should help us conserve our flashlight batteries. Any bright ideas for escape?'

'None worth mentioning,' said Birch.

'We could look for another entrance,' said Linka.

'I haven't seen anything.'

'Maybe it's another secret entrance.'

'Then how will we find it?' asked Birch. 'The last one was an accident.'

They sat silently. Hermux watched the dancing mouse with heartsick fascination. It was undoubtedly one of the masterpieces of watchmaker's art. Hinkum had desecrated it without a second thought and then left it to be destroyed.

He had an idea.

'There must be another way to get in here, because the scorpion must have been able to come and go. He looked pretty well fed to me. And if the lower entrances were buried in sand, then the other entrance must be up here somewhere. Linka, you saw some kind of cistern on top, didn't you?'

'Yes. Very close to the stairs.'

'I think they may have used that somehow to provide power for the dancer.'

'You mean cats were generating electricity three thousand years ago?'

'No. Something much simpler. Like a waterwheel.'

'But there's no water up there,' Birch interjected. 'There's nothing but sand.'

'You're right,' admitted Hermux. Then a smile crept slowly over his face. 'You're absolutely right! There's nothing but sand! Miles and miles of it!'

'But then, where would they get water?'

'Don't you see?' Hermux's voice rose with excitement. He fairly shouted, 'They didn't need water! They used sand. This entire thing is like a giant hourglass! Ouch!' He touched his sore lip carefully.

241

'You could be right,' said Linka. 'Remember the bulletin board in the workers' lounge? Urns are to be emptied promptly on the hour! That explains why the urns downstairs were filled with sand. The mice had to cart the sand away to keep the library from filling up. They carried it up the stairs and poured it back into the cistern.'

Hermux crawled up on to the stage with the now headless dancer.

'The machinery that operates this must be backstage,' he announced. 'If I'm right, then there should be a paddle wheel or some kind of drive mechanism that was turned by falling sand.'

Hermux made his way carefully through a shadowy tangle of rods and cables. Ahead of him he could make out the familiar outlines of a large, blocky machine. Then he recognized it. He already knew it by heart. He could draw it from memory. He had done so many times. Mirnikin Stepfitchler's original clock. It was in every watchmaking textbook. Every encyclopedia. 'He must have found a drawing of this and built it,' thought Hermux. 'What a fraud!'

'Is there anything there?' called Linka.

'Just a minute!' A driveshaft extended from the clock through a hole in the rear wall. 'Come on! I think I've found it.'

Just to the side of the driveshaft was a mouse-sized door. It was open.

When Linka and Birch had joined him, Hermux led the way.

'Be careful,' Birch cautioned him. 'Scorpions sometimes live in colonies.'

'Birch, that is totally disgusting!' Hermux said. He took a deep breath and stepped inside.

The fading light of the flashlight revealed the bottom of a shaft that rose straight up into the rock. Standing in the centre

242

was a wheel ringed with metal paddles just like Hermux had imagined. But far more important than that were the stairs that were cut into the walls.

'All right!' said Hermux. 'Let's get out of here!'

They crept silently up the stairs, listening for any sound of movement ahead. At last they came to the top, a landing with a low stone doorway. It was open just a crack. Outside at eye level they could see moonlight.

But the door wouldn't budge. It was half buried in sand.

Chapter 73
DESPERATE MEASURES

'I could dig us out, if I could reach it,' said Birch.

'Maybe we can blast our way out,' said Hermux.

'Excellent idea!' said Linka. 'We've got plenty of dynamite. Do you know how to use it?'

'No.'

'Birch?'

'No.'

'How hard can it be if Hinkum can do it?' Linka asked.

'You're right,' said Hermux. 'There's still a little fuse left. The question is, how much dynamite should we use? We don't want to blow ourselves up.'

'How about one stick?' said Birch. 'How much damage could that do?'

'Good. One stick it is. I'll go and get it. You figure out where we should put it.'

Back in the king's chamber, Hermux found the stick of dynamite that Hinkum had prepared. The blasting cap was inserted into one end of it. He picked up the burned-out stub of fuse and fitted it in the cap. Then he took the lantern and climbed carefully back up on to the stage. He stopped and looked back at the king and the mouse.

'This may be goodbye for all of us,' he said. 'But I'm very glad I lived to see you. Both of you.'

Birch and Linka had used one of the flashlights to tamp a hole in the sand outside, near the base of the door. The stick of dynamite fitted it perfectly.

'How do we light it?' asked Birch.

'I brought the lantern.'

'The fuse isn't very long, is it?' said Linka. 'How much time do you think it gives us?'

'Maybe thirty seconds,' said Birch. 'Tops.'

'I'll light it,' said Hermux. 'You two wait at the bottom of the stairs.'

'You're sure?' asked Linka.

'I can be very fast when I want to,' Hermux boasted, trying to convince himself as well as them. 'Let me know when you're ready.'

'All right then,' called Birch when he and Linka reached the bottom of the stairs. 'Light her up. And run like the dickens!'

Hermux set the lamp on the floor and pushed it closer and closer to the fuse. The flame sputtered and dimmed.

'Don't die on me now,' he begged. He turned up the wick and the flame flared again. He picked up the end of the fuse and slid it very slowly into the lantern's vent at the top of the chimney.

Then he held his breath and watched.

A thin wisp of smoke drifted from the lantern. Hermux started towards the stairs. He stood on the top step and waited.

He thought he could see a tiny red glow. Then a jolt of adrenalin shot through him as sparks began to fly.

'I'm on my way!' he shouted. Then he ran like he never had before.

It was only centrifugal force that kept him from falling as he corkscrewed down the shaft. When he bounced to the bottom, he made two full circuits around the room before Birch grabbed him and yanked him out the door, slamming it shut just before the explosion.

There was a dull boom. The shock wave blew the door off its hinges.

Chapter 74

DOWN AND OUT

The dynamite worked. The door was gone. Along with the roof. And most of the wall. And the top two steps.

'Let me go first,' said Linka. She gauged the distance before leaping up gracefully. She extended her hand back to Hermux and Birch. 'Come on. It's not bad.'

They clambered up beside her and stepped gratefully out on to the sand.

'This is the cistern,' said Linka. 'It's not far from here to the steps.'

After the closeness of the tomb the chilly air smelled wonderfully fresh. Hermux took a deep breath. He knelt and scooped up a handful of sand and watched it trickle through his fingers.

'Simple but ingenious,' he mused. 'The sand was held here and then released to fall down through the shaft to the sand-wheel. It's wonderful, really. Direct and to the point.'

Hermux scratched his ear furiously for a moment. Then he stopped to examine himself. His throat felt bruised from the scorpion's pincer. His burned lip was swollen and painful. One of the sleeves of his jacket had been ripped to shreds by the wall of the stairwell. His arm ached. He was filthy. His tail was nicked in several places, and it had a long scrape towards the tip. But he was still in one piece. He gave a brisk shake and heaved a sigh of relief.

'That was really a close call,' he said.

'One of the closest,' said Linka, who still looked fresh and composed despite the sand in her fur and a smudge of tomb dust on her snout.

'Too close!' said Birch grumpily. He rubbed the lump on his head. 'I may be getting too old for this. Could we just sit down for minute?'

'There's no reason to hurry now,' said Hermux. 'We've got all the time in the world.'

'But what about Tucka?' asked Linka. 'We've got to save her!'

'We do?' asked Birch.

Hermux shook his head. 'I completely forgot Tucka. Linka's right. We've got to save her. She is vain and selfish and mean. And she probably wouldn't lift a finger to save us.'

'We know that for a fact!' Linka interjected.

'But she doesn't deserve to die. Especially at the hands of a worthless sneak like Hinkum Stepfitchler the Third.'

'Sounds like poetic justice to me,' said Birch.

'Birch, that just doesn't sound like you,' scolded Linka.

'You're right. I'm sorry. Being selfish isn't a capital offence. And anyway, after getting a second chance for myself, how could I deny one for someone else? But what can we do?'

'First, let's get back to the plane,' said Linka. 'Follow me. We'll use the stairs down the canyon wall.'

★ ★ ★

248

To their relief the plane appeared to be untouched. But when Linka pressed the starter button, nothing happened.

She pressed it again.

'Drat!' she said. 'I'll bet Hinkum took the distributor.'

'Oh, no!' said Hermux in dismay. 'What can we do now?'

'I suppose I could put in the spare,' said Linka cheerfully. 'Come on! It's fun. You can help. Lucky for us that Hinkum is a little amateurish at this villain thing. Like I've never been through the missing distributor before. Villain lesson number one: never underestimate your opponent. A professional villain would have blown up the plane!'

'He was certainly willing to blow us up,' said Hermux.

'Willing ... but not able. There's a big difference.'

★ ★ ★

'OK. That ought to do it,' she said. 'Stand back. Birch, try the engine.'

It turned over and started immediately.

'All right,' she shouted. 'Let's get this baby in the air.'

Minutes later they were bumping their way down the sandy floor of the canyon. Hermux tightened his seat belt another notch as the plane gathered speed. He tapped Linka on the shoulder.

'Are you sure you can do this in the dark?' he asked.

'I don't have much choice, do I?' she replied.

Chapter 75
BY INVITATION ONLY

'Sorry. No admittance.' The skinny gopher spread his arms to block the gangway. 'It's a private party.'

'We know that,' said Linka impatiently. 'We're guests. Why do you think we're here?'

He scrutinized her dirty face and Hermux's torn and tattered clothes. 'You're not dressed for a wedding,' he observed dryly.

'Of course not!' she said in an exasperated tone. 'We've been travelling all day. We'd like to get on board and change before the ceremony.'

'Wait a minute,' he said. A light dawned in his dull face. 'There aren't any guests! I remember now. Mr Stepfitchler said so.'

'What kind of wedding doesn't have any guests?' Hermux demanded.

'I didn't want to have to say this . . .' Linka began in a softer tone, 'but you're right. We're not guests in the usual sense. I'm Moozella Corkin –'

'*The* Moozella Corkin?' the gopher asked in astonishment. 'The gossip columnist?'

'That's me.' Linka winked. 'This is my assistant, Trevin.' She nodded toward Hermux. Then she pointed to Birch. 'And this is my photographer, Filch. And what is your name?'

'Blurt.'

'Blurt, we're in a ticklish situation here. Miss Mertslin sold my paper the exclusive rights to her wedding. In fact, we paid her a lot of money.'

She whispered in his ear.

'Oh my gosh!' Blurt said.

'It's all a big surprise for Mr Stepfitchler. The arrangements were very last minute. As you can see, we barely got here in time.'

'How did you get here?' asked the puzzled gopher.

'Speedboat,' said Hermux.

'Oh.' The gopher nodded. Then he stiffened. 'Sorry. I still can't let you aboard. I've got strict orders.'

'Have you ever done any modelling, Blurt?' asked Linka. 'You've got a very striking face. Great jawline. Filch, be sure to get a couple of shots of Blurt before we go. Now, as I was saying, Blurt.' She became very serious. 'We paid Tucka an extravagantly large sum of money. And if we don't get to cover her wedding, she's going to have to refund the paper's money. Every penny of it. Have you ever seen Tucka get angry?'

'Yes, ma'am, I have,' he said nervously.

'It's not very pretty, is it?'

'No, ma'am, it's not.'

'You'd probably rather not have her angry at you.'

'No, ma'am, I wouldn't.'

'Do you think she'd be angry if she found out that it was your fault that she's not on the front page of the paper? And on top of that, she owes us a lot of money?'

'She'd be very angry.'

'I don't want that. Do you?'

'No, ma'am, I don't.'

'Then I think we'd better come aboard.' Linka began walking up the gangway. She motioned for Hermux and Birch to follow her.

Blurt stepped aside.

'All right,' he said. 'If you're sure this is what she wants.'

'I'm sure,' Linka said sweetly. 'And don't worry. Tucka will sort everything out with Mr Stepfitchler. She's got him wrapped around her little finger.'

Linka stopped and turned back to him. 'Oh, incidentally, where is the crew right now? I'd love to get a few shots of them before the ceremony to get the flavour of life on a showboat.'

'Hardly anyone's left. Mr Stepfitchler let most of the crew go yesterday. Right now they're probably all in the galley getting drunk. Drinks are on the house tonight.'

'Thank you,' she said, pinching his cheek lightly. 'And don't let us leave without getting your picture. I just know you've got a big future in fashion.'

Chapter 76
LAST-MINUTE JITTERS

'Are you nervous, sweetie?' Hinkum smiled as he poured Tucka a glass of red clover wine.

'Just a little,' she admitted. She lifted her veil to sip her wine. 'I wish Rink could have been here. I know he would have done something remarkable with the candles and the flowers. And I know you love your privacy, but I would have liked just a few guests. Close friends. Although there's not much room left with this crate. It certainly is imposing. I'm just dying to see what's in it! I can't believe you just marched off and got it! Just like that! The gold statue of a cat king.'

'I did. And it's spectacular. You won't be disappointed.'

'You're amazing!'

'I am.'

'That chipmunk fellow of Mirrin's looked for twenty years.'

'Forty.'

'Forty years. And he didn't find a thing. And you found it in one afternoon.'

'Call me lucky.'

'I'd rather call you Hinky.'

'You know I don't like that.'

The boat lurched slightly.

'We're casting off,' said Hinkum. 'I want to get closer to the falls. We'll have a spectacular view.'

'You know, Hinky, I've been thinking,' Tucka sighed. 'Dead Rat Falls is not a very pretty name, is it. Not for a wedding memory.'

'No, I guess it isn't, now that you mention it.'

'Wouldn't it be so much better if it were renamed something lovely? Like "Tucka's Wedding Veil"? Doesn't that sound nice?'

'It would take some doing.'

'But you're Hinkum Stepfitchler. Didn't your great-great-great-great-grandfather or whatever invent geography? Can't you just get the name changed?'

'It's not quite that easy.'

'Oh, Hinky! You own a university, for goodness' sake! What's the point, if they can't even change the name of a waterfall? It would make me so happy! And we could announce it when we announce the wedding and the museum.'

Hinkum seemed about to give in when the captain appeared.

'Shall we begin the ceremony?' he enquired. 'Where would you and your bride like to stand?'

'How about here, near the railing?' answered Hinkum. 'That will give us the best view of the falls.'

Tucka joined Hinkum at the railing. She looked quite regal in her balloon-shaped, white chenille gown. Except for impossibly long artificial eyelashes, she wore very little make-up, only a touch of lavender lipstick and a little black patent rouge on her nose. She had tied fluffy lavender satin bows the entire length of her tail, and they fluttered gaily in the breeze from the falls.

'Dear friends,' the captain began.

Tucka gazed fondly at the wedding cake. It was a triumph of

254

decorative baking. A small bride and groom stood atop the towering construction of flour and frosting. It was an exact replica of Rink Firsheen's plans for the Tucka Mertslin Museum of Monumental Art. She brushed away a tear. This was a beautiful moment. It irked her that there was no press coverage.

'We are gathered here tonight to join, in holy matrimony, two lovely people, Tucka Mertslin and Hinkum Stepfitchler the Third ...'

Hermux crept to the edge of the crate and peered around the corner. He motioned for Linka and Birch to move forward.

'And now, Tucka,' concluded the captain, 'do you take Hinkum Stepfitchler the Third to be your lawful wedded husband, in sickness and in health, for rich or for poor, until death do you part? Signify by saying, "I do."'

'Don't do it, Tucka!' Hermux shouted as he leapt out from behind the crate. 'It's a trick!'

'Who is that?' demanded Tucka, squinting in the candlelight.

'It's Hermux. Hermux Tantamoq!'

'Tantamoq? Tantamoq? You weren't invited!' She stepped protectively between Hermux and the cake.

'Of course I wasn't! We're here to save your life!'

'Tantamoq!' said Hinkum in a strained voice.

'Surprised to see us?' Hermux sneered.

'Well, of course I am,' Hinkum said, recovering his composure. 'Naturally it's a surprise to see you so far from home. But it's always a pleasure to bump into someone from Pinchester. And your friends are with you?'

'We certainly are!' said Linka, stepping out to face him.

'Tucka, he's only marrying you for your money,' Birch explained.

'That's ridiculous!' she sputtered. 'He's a Stepfitchler!'

'He's planning to kill you,' Linka told her.

'Nonsense! We're starting a museum together.'

'There won't be any museum, Tucka. That crate is full of nothing but rocks.'

The captain looked confused. 'Should I go on?' he asked Hinkum.

'Of course. Go on! These people are deranged. Tucka darling, it's time for you to say, "I do."'

'Don't do it, Tucka!' It was Linka talking. 'He's no good. You've got to trust us!'

Tucka seemed to hesitate.

'Mrs Hinkum Stepfitchler the Third! Just think of the way it sounds,' Hinkum urged her. 'Just say it with me one time. Mrs Hinkum Stepfitchler the Third ...'

'Mrs Hinkum Stepfitchler the Third ... I do like the way it sounds! It's got music to it!'

'More than music,' said Hinkum. 'It's a name fit for a queen. For you, Tucka! Your own dynasty! Think of the way it will look in print. "Mrs Hinkum Stepfitchler the Third hosted the party of the season at her palatial home on the campus of exclusive Stepfitchler University. Everyone who is anyone was there." Think of Elusa Loitavender's face when she reads that in the newspaper.'

A smile played about Tucka's lips.

'Oh,' she said, 'I can just picture it. All right ... I ...'

'Have you actually seen what's in the crate, Tucka?' Hermux demanded. 'There's no statue in there. There's nothing but rocks. Rocks to weigh down your body when he throws you overboard, so he can inherit all your money.'

'Hinkum!' Tucka scowled. 'I know you're a very naughty mouse, but that's going too far.'

'It's nonsense, Tucka,' Hinkum assured her. 'Just the ravings of a jealous lunatic, a nobody, a watchmaker. And a broken-down failure of a professor.'

'Just look inside the crate!' Linka insisted.

'Well, I don't suppose one little peek would hurt,' Tucka said.

'No, Tucka,' Hinkum said. 'I can't allow that. A marriage is built on trust. If you don't trust me, how can we have a lasting relationship?'

'I do trust you, Hinkum. But it's my statue. And it's my museum. I just want a peek!'

'No peeking! Not until after the wedding.'

'But I want to see it!'

'Keep your hands off! It's a wedding present. It's not yours until the wedding is over! Just say "I do" and you'll get everything that's coming to you!'

But Tucka was beginning to feel stubborn.

'You promised me a gold statue,' she complained. 'A big one. Twenty-four carat! You promised, and I want to see it!'

Hinkum reached into the pocket of his tuxedo and withdrew a very small, very black revolver.

'Step away from the crate, Tucka, and say it! Say "I do"!'

Tucka stared at him in astonishment.

'This is very irregular,' said the captain, who had been waiting patiently for Tucka to make up her mind. 'Maybe she doesn't want to marry you.'

Hinkum pointed the gun casually at the captain and smiled unpleasantly.

'And then again, maybe she does,' said the captain. 'Come on, darlin', lots of people get cold feet at the last minute. I've seen it hundreds of times. Just take a deep breath and say "I do".'

Tucka looked at Hinkum again. He gave her a devilish smile and winked.

'Oh, Hinkum, you're a very, very bad boy. And I ought to punish you for this. But I just can't say no to you.' She took a deep breath.

'You'll be sorry, Tucka!' yelled Hermux.

Hinkum pointed the gun at Hermux.

'Oh, Hinkum!' gushed Tucka. 'You'd really kill for me, wouldn't you? That is so sweet. But no bloodshed at the wedding. I want to remember it as a very special day.'

'OK! OK!' said Hinkum, lowering the gun slightly. 'But let's get on with it.'

'Did he tell you that he's completely broke?' asked Linka. 'Not a single dime! Nothing! Who paid for this boat, Tucka? Who's paying for the wedding?'

'Hinkum, that's not true, is it? You're not really broke, are you?'

'What difference does it make? Now say it! I command you! You're my wife! You have to do what I tell you!'

'You're right,' said Tucka, suddenly seeming to crumble. She made a tiny curtsy towards Hinkum and bowed her head demurely. 'Except for one small detail,' she muttered. 'We're not married yet!'

Tucka's foot shot out from beneath her wedding dress in a lightning-fast high kick. Hinkum's gun flew up into the air, bounced across the deck and dropped into the river with a splash.

'In case you're still wondering,' she growled, 'the answer is no! The wedding is off!'

Hermux, Birch and Linka formed a flying wedge and rushed Hinkum, knocking him flat on the deck.

258

Tucka ran to the crate. She ripped off the gigantic red bow and pried the side open.

'Rocks!' she screamed furiously. 'Rocks! Hinkum, you rotten worm!'

She marched over to the wedding cake. She grabbed the groom off the top and bit his head off. She spat it over the rail.

'There!' she said. She set the bride down carefully in a bouquet of white roses and baby's breath. Then she lifted the entire wedding cake and carried it to where Hinkum lay sprawled, trying to catch his breath.

'Mrs Hinkum Stepfitchler the Third requests the pleasure of your company for an evening of fun and games,' she announced. 'Refreshments will be served!'

Then she dropped the cake on his head.

Chapter 77
SPRING IS IN THE AIR

Hermux finished polishing the crystal on Tratin Dilmo's wristwatch and placed it carefully in a dark green box embossed with the words

Hermux Tantamoq, Watchmaker.

Then he placed the box on the WILL CALL shelf and stood looking out of the front window at Ferbosh Avenue.

'April must be the loveliest month for watchmaking!' thought Hermux. 'Just look at all those daffodils!'

There must have been a dozen big pots of daffodils on the pavement in front of the Tentriff Academy of Dance and Theatrics.

'Next spring I'm going to have flowers in front of my shop,' Hermux thought. 'It really does brighten things up.'

The door to the shop burst open, and in strode Lista Blenwipple with the morning mail.

'Good morning, Hermux!' she said. Lista smiled broadly as she handed him the bundle of bills and catalogues.

Hermux began to remove the rubber band.

'Oh, forget all that stuff!' said Lista. 'A bunch of worthless junk. Here's the real thing.' She withdrew a familiar pale grey envelope and placed it ceremoniously on the counter.

'Open it!' she commanded.

Hermux slit it open carefully and removed the card inside.

The Department of Modern Art of the
Pinchester Museum of Art and Science
requests the honour of your presence
for the gala opening of

THE TUCKA MERTSLIN GALLERY
OF MONUMENTAL ART
KA-NARSH-PAH:
THE LEGACY OF A FORGOTTEN PEOPLE

Findings of the historic Perflinger-Tentintrotter Expedition
The Sands of Time: An installation by
Hermux Tantamoq, Watchmaker

April 12   8 p.m.

Formal Attire • Dinner • Dancing • R. S. V. P.

'Now you're famous!' she crowed. 'And I see that you've read the paper this morning. I don't suppose you read Moozella Corkin's column? Elusa Loitavender and Professor Turfip Dandiffer announce their June wedding? Does that ring a bell?'

'I think I did hear something about it,' said Hermux, feigning indifference.

'I should say you did,' scoffed Lista. 'And from the horse's mouth, I expect. How did Linka find out? Was there an awful fight?'

'No. There wasn't any fight. When we got back from the desert, she and Turfip had a long talk. It was mutual.'

'Not what I heard,' countered Lista. 'Although I hate to rely on that scatterbrain Lanayda Prink for information. But Lanayda says that your friend Mirrin Stentrill practically threw Elusa and Turfip into each other's arms at an intimate little dinner party of hers while you and Linka were off on your adventure.'

'No. It wasn't intimate. Mirrin just invited some of the museum board members over to her studio to see her new paintings. And there was a little informal dinner afterwards. And Mirrin had invited Turfip because she thought he might be lonely, with Linka being out of town and all. Then apparently one thing led to another. And when we got back, Turfip broke off the engagement with Linka. It seems that Elusa understands him much more than Linka. And she's very interested in supporting his career. And it didn't seem like Linka really had her heart in it. And our adventure just proved that to him. Besides all that, although he didn't feel entirely comfortable mentioning it, Elusa Loitavender has financial resources and social connections that could be very advantageous for a professor who wants to make a name for himself.'

'What did Linka say to that?'

'She didn't get to say much of anything. Turfip's speech took up most of the evening. She returned his ring, and he left. Luckily she had kept his ring in a safe place, so it wasn't all dinged up.'

Chapter 78
HIGH SIGN

Tucka hummed contentedly as her limousine pushed its way towards the museum steps.

The crowd tonight was even bigger than the crowd for Mirrin's show. And much better behaved. Everyone wanted to see the cat king. People had been talking about nothing else for weeks.

Tucka had made sure of that. It had been just one more detail in a very busy winter. First of all, she had funded an entire new wing for the museum to house the Ka-Narsh-Pah collection. She had hired Rink Firsheen to design it. He had flown out immediately and stayed with her on the showboat while he did drawings of the library and the tomb and worked up new plans. Then she had paid, and paid handsomely, to have the golden mummy and the dancing mouse carefully removed from the tomb and shipped to Pinchester. She had even hired Hermux Tantamoq himself to restore the dancing mouse to working order. On top of that, she had made peace with Ortolina Perriflot. Together they had established a foundation to purchase the Stepfitchler Mansion and the entire contents of its underground library. They had appointed Birch Tentintrotter to head the foundation and to create an institute for the study of Ancient Cat. It had been an extremely expensive winter.

'But it was still cheaper than marrying Stepfitchler,' she had told Skimpy Dormay.

And of course there was Stepfitchler's trial. Poor blundering fool. If she had been Hinkum, she would have made sure the dynamite had gone off. Well, luckily for her, he didn't have her instinct for follow-through. Naturally she had been the star witness against him. At his sentencing, she had appeared as the tragic widow. Even though they weren't married and he wasn't dead. Still, she was in mourning. He had broken her heart, after all. Although now that she had taken a good look around the Stepfitchler Mansion, she was relieved to be rid of him. What a dreary dump that turned out to be. She would have had to tear it down and start over. Building a museum wing had been much easier and more fun.

'Yes,' she thought. 'It has all turned out quite nicely.' The new fragrance was selling like gangbusters. She had even taken a billboard for it directly across from the museum. As she stepped from the limo and waved graciously at the crowd, she felt on top of the world.

After she signed a few autographs, she couldn't resist turning to see her billboard. It was smashing. There she was – as bright as day on the top of an apartment building. She was two fabulous storeys tall and dressed in the same gold lamé halter top and silk harem pants that she was wearing tonight. She knelt before a towering golden statue of a cat. Her pose spoke of humility, but her eyes smouldered with passion.

Slave!

**The powerful new fragrance
from Tucka Mertslin**

Let him know who's boss!

Chapter 79
LABOUR OF LOVE

Mayor Pinkwiggin was just wrapping up his speech.

'I've always said that Pinchester is a big-hearted city, and now we've got the big art to prove it! Let's bring out the remarkable woman that made this all possible. Your friend and mine. Pinchester's own beauty queen ... Tucka Mertslin.'

Tucka took the microphone with a flourish.

'Friends, art lovers and fellow Pinchesterians, as you all know by now, nothing gives me more pleasure than an act of enormous generosity. So you can imagine how wonderful it is for me to welcome you here this evening.'

The mayor handed her an enormous pair of scissors. Tucka snipped through the broad red ribbon in one cut.

'Ladies and gentlemen!' she declared. 'I give you the Tucka Mertslin Gallery of Monumental Art!'

A gong sounded. The heavy bronze doors slowly swung open. The crowd pushed forward into the gallery. They were anticipating something remarkable.

They were not disappointed. Rink Firsheen had designed a stunning setting for the king's mummy, modelled after the tomb.

The soaring stone walls sloped in slightly, creating an even grander sense of height. On a raised dais of plum-coloured sandstone sat Ka-Narsh-Pah, Eye-of-Heaven, Talon-of-Justice, Strength-of-Many, Merciful-Paw and Father-of-All. He greeted the populace of Pinchester with an expression of timeless serenity.

'Oh!' someone said, breaking the stunned silence that settled over the room.

'Oh my!' said someone else.

'Oh my goodness!' said a third.

'It's bigger than I thought.'

'It's huge.'

'Are they sure it's dead?'

Then everyone spoke at once.

It was some time before anyone noticed what Ka-Narsh-Pah was looking at.

The wall opposite the king was covered by a midnight blue velvet curtain embroidered with tiny gold and silver stars. At the far end of the room stood an enormous apparatus. A set of stone stairs was built against the wall. At the top of the stairs an enormous copper funnel was bolted to the wall. Beneath the funnel was what looked like the paddle wheel of a steamboat. Below that on the floor was a large mound of sand.

Tucka tapped her microphone.

'Friends, is this fabulous or what? Wouldn't you just love to be buried like this? All this space just for you and with hundreds of people visiting you every day? Plus a gift shop? And postcards? Being dead wouldn't be so bad. But seriously, I want to introduce some of the people that helped make this remarkable tribute to art and science a reality. First of all, Professor

Birch Tentintrotter, who, as you all know by now, played a part in the discovery of the library and the tomb. Professor Tentintrotter?'

Birch took the microphone from Tucka. He looked over at Mirrin. She smiled at him. Her eyes were brimming with tears.

'Thank you very much. But before I begin, I want to thank the most wonderful woman in the world. Without her faith in me, none of this could have happened. I believe you all know her. Mirrin Stentrill.'

There was a smattering of polite applause. And quite a bit of whispering.

'I think the easiest way to explain what you're about to see is to read to you the text of a scroll that was found in the base of Ka-Narsh-Pah's mummy when we removed it from his tomb. It was written in Cat more than three thousand years ago. I hope you'll excuse the roughness of the translation. I'm sure we will improve upon it in the years to come. I have titled it

The Tragic History of the King and the Dancer

Once upon a time, there lived a young slavemouse who loved to dance. She danced at home. She danced in the village. She danced in the sunlight with golden bells on her wrists. She danced in the moonlight with silver bells on her ankles. She danced in the spring when the river rose. She danced in the autumn when it receded. She danced in the summer when the work was hard. She danced in the autumn when the harvest was done. Everyone who saw her dance was moved by her beauty, her grace and her joy.

Now the kingdom was ruled by a powerful king, who was greatly loved by his people. Ka-Narsh-Pah had fought many wars and defeated

many enemies. But he had grown weary and sad and tired of living. His court had grown weary and sad with him. Music and laughter were never heard. Faces were long. And days were dreary.

One day the prime minister heard about the young dancing slave-mouse. He resolved to have her dance before the king.

'If she brings joy to everyone who sees her dance, perhaps she can bring joy to the king,' he thought.

The prime minister summoned the dancing girl and commanded her to dance that night at the king's birthday banquet.

Unlike most birthday parties, this one was not happy. The king sat at the head of the table, looking downcast. He did not seem pleased by his presents. He did not say thank you for the new crown. Or the golden chariot. Or the jewelled throne. He did not say anything at all. No one else could think of anything to say either.

They didn't even sing 'Happy Birthday'.

It was into this silent party that the young dancer shyly walked. Her gold and silver bells tinkled merrily. The prime minister watched the king nervously.

The king looked up, surprised at the musical sound. Then he saw the young dancer wrapped in veils. He smiled in surprise. He really was a handsome king when he smiled. All the guests smiled with him. Especially the prime minister.

The drummer struck the rhythm. The dancer closed her eyes. Then she began to tap her foot and sway. At the sound of the harp, she raised her arms and began to turn, moving slowly at first and then faster and faster. She moved smoothly across the great stone floor. She circled the banquet table. She clapped her hands gaily. She stamped her feet in time to the sinuous drumbeats. She moved like water. Like the wind. Like clouds drifting across the sky. She whirled. She ran. She leapt high into the air and landed lightly on one foot. And there she balanced as the music came to a stop.

269

The king was captivated.

'Tell her to come closer,' he said.

The prime minister motioned her forward. She stood before the king and bowed deeply, breathless with exertion and with the excitement of being at court and dancing before the king.

'You have made me very happy,' he told her. 'Happier than I have been in many years. Will you stay here at the palace and dance for me every day?'

She said yes.

From that day forward the little dancer lived at the palace and danced for the king. He called for her if he was sad, and she danced for him. If he was happy, he called for her.

He grew to love her very much.

He offered to marry her and make her his queen.

She accepted, but on one condition. The king must free all her people from slavery.

He agreed. He would make a proclamation on their wedding day.

When the king's subjects heard this, some of them were very angry.

How could a cat marry a mouse? How could a mouse be queen? Who would do all the work if the slaves were freed?

It was just the opportunity the king's brother, Da-Harsh-Pah, had been waiting for.

He was tired of being assistant king. He wanted to be king.

On the eve of the marriage, he took a present to the dancing mouse.

'I have brought you a beautiful gold brush to brush your fur before your wedding.'

The dancing mouse thanked him. That night, before she went to bed, she brushed her fur very carefully.

The brush was poisoned. In the morning she was found dead. There were rumours about the king's brother, but the king was too stricken by grief to hear or speak to anyone.

He didn't cry. But he never laughed or smiled again. He seldom spoke. He lost all interest in being king. He forgot about his subjects. He forgot about freeing the slaves.

He left his palace and retired to his library at the edge of the desert. But he had no taste for reading. No taste for food. He sat motionless in the darkness and thought only of the dancer and the dark and cold emptiness that had taken her place.

In desperation the prime minister assembled the court.

'What can we do?' he asked.

'Restore the king's delight!'

And so the command was given to the master of mechanisms. He locked himself in his workshop and set to work. He laboured day and night on a mysterious mechanism the likes of which had never been seen before. He barely ate or slept. And finally it was done.

The machine was disassembled and taken up the river on a royal barge to the king's library. The master of mechanisms reassembled it, and the king was called. The once mighty Ka-Narsh-Pah, whose voice alone vanquished enemies, was now too weak to walk. He was carried on a litter.

The master of mechanisms bent low before him and begged forgiveness in advance, if his efforts failed to please the king.

But when the king saw what the master of mechanisms had created, he was very pleased indeed. Tears of grief and happiness flowed readily from his eyes.

And for the remainder of his days, he recalled, if only faintly, the happiness that had once been his.'

When Birch finished, there were more than a few muffled sobs in the audience.

Mirrin dabbed her eyes with a hanky. Tucka checked her

watch. This was taking up a lot more time than she had thought – time that might be better used admiring her gallery.

'Thank you, Professor Tentintrotter. It's just one more example of the incredible power of real beauty. And now I'd like to introduce my dear friend and neighbour, Mr Hermux Tantamoq, who also assisted in the discovery of the tomb and who has worked for the past several months, with the generous financial support of Tucka Mertslin Cosmetics, to restore an important part of the discovery to its original beauty. I'm going to turn the programme over to Mr Tantamoq, who I hope will not bore us all with a long speech.'

She eyed Hermux sternly as she handed him the microphone. There was a small burst of applause.

'Thank you, everybody,' said Hermux nervously. 'I don't have a lot to say except that this was really a labour of love. For me. For the master of mechanisms. And especially for King Ka-Narsh-Pah.'

Hermux walked over to the sand pile and removed a metal scoop from a basket filled with scoops. He filled it with sand.

'Now are there any children here?' he asked. 'I need some volunteers.'

A dozen tiny paws went up.

'If each of you would fill up one of these scoops and follow me ... and if the rest of you would line up behind them.'

He climbed the stone stairs with the children right behind him. He emptied his scoop into the broad mouth of the copper funnel. A fine steady stream of sand began to fall from the narrow opening at its bottom.

He motioned for the children to do the same. Then he descended the stairs and handed his scoop to the first person in line. That was Tucka, naturally. And then the mayor. Then the mayor's wife. And his son. Then Flurty Palin. And Skimpy Dormay. And Elusa Loitavender. And Turfip Dandiffer. And Birkanny Denteel. Then came Mirrin and Birch and Linka. Linka patted him warmly on the shoulder as she went by.

'Good job, Hermux!' she told him.

The sand continued to fall. It struck the vanes of the wheel below it, setting it into motion, before returning to its mound on the floor. The wheel turned a shaft. The shaft turned the escape wheel that Birch had found. The escape wheel set the pendulum in motion and turned a small gear. That gear turned another that was connected to a series of wheels that turned cams and shoved rods and pulled wires that disappeared behind the stage. As the machine began to whir, the starry blue curtain slowly began to part.

'Ladies and gentlemen,' Hermux announced, 'I present to you the King's Delight.'

From offstage came the sound of small cymbals and a drum.

Then with a leap that caused everyone to gasp in amazement, the beautiful young mechanical mouse leapt on to the stage.

Hermux had repaired her head. He had replaced her eye. He had polished her enamelled fur. He had cleaned and oiled every gear. Adjusted each rod and cable. Fine-tuned the timing.

She was magical. So light that her feet barely touched the ground. So quick that she seemed to be everywhere at once. Her brilliant eyes flashed. Her spangled arms jangled. Her tail moved in perfect harmony, countering the thrust of her legs and the tilt of her head.

For Pinchester, as it had been for King Ka-Narsh-Pah, it was love at first sight.

Chapter 80
GOODBYES

A small gallery to the side of Ka-Narsh-Pah told the story of
Birch's discovery, beginning with his finding of the first map
in the Rare Books Library at Stepfitchler University. It included his journals and notebooks, detailed maps of the
Longish River Valley, and, spotlighted in their own glass case,
Prowlah Paad's scroll and the bronze escape wheel that had
saved Hermux's life.

The gallery also displayed Mirrin's most recent painting.
She had titled it *Four Friends*.

The painting showed three mice and a chipmunk having a
picnic in a grassy field. The sun is bright. The remains of a big
lunch are strewn across the orange and blue checked tablecloth.
Loaves of bread, creamy white cheese, a bunch of grapes, a bottle of dandelion wine. Glasses sparkle in the light.

In the painting Birch is explaining something. His face is
animated. One paw is held up to emphasize his point.

Linnix Tantamoq is lying on his back with his knees up, listening to Birch, and gazing up at the sky. His wife, Tirrathee, is
leaning against his knees. She has pale grey fur. She is wearing
a large sun hat and reading a book. It is a happy moment of bal-

ance and harmony. In the midst of it, Mirrin shades her eyes and looks directly out at the viewer, as though to say, 'You and I must remember this moment for the rest of our lives.'

Mirrin found Hermux standing in front of the painting. He was lost in thought.

'Your mother and father would be very proud of you,' she said quietly. 'I know that Birch and I are.'

'She looks so young,' Hermux said, pointing to his mother.

'We were all young, Hermux. So full of hope. And look how things have turned out. Not so bad really. But not anything like what we expected.'

'I am really happy for you and Birch,' Hermux told her. He put his arms around her and hugged her to him. 'And I haven't thanked you yet for your matchmaking efforts with Turfip.'

'Oh, that was nothing.' Mirrin chuckled. 'He seemed like an ambitious mouse to me. And Elusa has always had a weakness for professor types. She and I have that in common.'

'I'm going to look for Birch,' Mirrin said. 'Why don't you join us?'

'I think I'll see if I can find Linka,' he demurred.

'Of course,' she said. She kissed him lightly on the cheek. 'Good luck!'

In the main gallery the crowd had thinned out. Linka stood by the stage, watching the dancing mouse execute a dazzling twirl.

'You did a wonderful job repairing her,' she told Hermux. 'It's ironic, isn't it? A king gave up his kingdom for her, but she doesn't even have a name. Do you think he really loved her?'

'Without a doubt,' said Hermux.

'A cat in love with a mouse. A king in love with one of his slaves. It's very romantic,' Linka mused. 'Although it would have been nice if he'd remembered to free the slaves.'

275

'True,' said Hermux. 'But then history would have been very different. You and I wouldn't be here. We would never have been born. And besides, from what Birch says, we didn't wait for the cats to free us. We freed ourselves.'

'We did, didn't we? Should we go look at the murals? They upset me so horribly when I saw them in the library. But I think I'm ready to see them now.'

Linka and Hermux walked down the long hallway into the narrow gallery that Rink Firsheen had designed for the murals. Overhead, golden stars twinkled on the dark blue vault of the ceiling. On the walls were the stately murals from the main reading room of Ka-Narsh-Pah's library. They had been meticulously removed and reinstalled. In scene after scene the sleek and luxurious lives of the cat people were supported by the endless industry of their mouse slaves.

The gallery was jammed with people. They moved slowly from image to image. Studying each one as though it were a revelation. It was a strangely quiet and thoughtful crowd for Pinchester. Even Tucka was at a loss for words.

Then a silvery mole in a green uniform rang a bell and announced, 'Ladies and gentlemen, dinner is now served!'

Mayor Pinkwiggin led the stampede. Flurty Palin was right on his heels. In moments the gallery was empty.

Linka and Hermux were alone.

'Well,' Hermux said, looking around the empty gallery, 'the show is over. I guess we should join the others.'

'Yes,' said Linka. 'I guess we should.'

'Although I was thinking ...'

'Yes?'

'I thought that maybe you and I,' Hermux stuttered, 'if you wanted to, of course, well, we might go somewhere and have

276

dinner together. Just the two of us. I know a quiet little restaurant that's not far from here.'

'Why, Hermux,' she said warmly, 'I'd love to.'

'You would?'

'Of course I would.'

'Then I guess we can go,' he said.

'I guess we can.' Linka smiled.

As they left, they waved goodbye to the cats and mice. They nodded to the mysterious mechanical dancer, who seemed to raise her hand in recognition before she began a series of graceful leaps across the stage. They stopped and bowed slightly to Ka-Narsh-Pah.

'Goodbye, old fellow!' said Hermux, remembering how awfully frightened he had been the first time he had seen him.

'It's been swell!' said Linka.

They walked across the Great Entry Hall and stepped through the revolving door out into the cool spring night.

'There's a bus!' said Hermux. 'Let's see if we can catch it.'

It was just beginning to rain – a light rain – the kind that daffodils in particular seem to like. Hermux took off his jacket and tried to hold it over their heads as they ran. It didn't do much good.

They caught up with the bus as it turned the corner, and they clambered on board.

'Goodness!' Linka laughed, looking at their reflections in the window. 'We're all wet! Are you cold?'

'No,' said Hermux. He gazed fondly at Linka's damp, furry face. 'I've never felt better in my life!'

In Memoriam

LIONEL
1983–2001

Thank you for the adventures,
for the laughter and for eighteen years
of unconditional friendship.